Sex with Strangers

Also by Michael Lowenthal

The Paternity Test

Charity Girl

Avoidance

The Same Embrace

Sex with Strangers

Michael Lowenthal

THE UNIVERSITY OF WISCONSIN PRESS

The University of Wisconsin Press
728 State Street, Suite 443
Madison, Wisconsin 53706
uwpress.wisc.edu

Gray's Inn House, 127 Clerkenwell Road
London EC1R 5DB, United Kingdom
eurospanbookstore.com

Printed in the United States of America
This book may be available in a digital edition.

Library of Congress Cataloging-in-Publication Data

Names: Lowenthal, Michael, author.
Title: Sex with strangers / Michael Lowenthal.
Description: Madison, Wisconsin : The University of Wisconsin Press, [2021]
Identifiers: LCCN 2020035410 | ISBN 9780299332648 (paperback)
Subjects: LCGFT: Short stories. | Fiction.
Classification: LCC PS3562.O894 S49 2021 | DDC 813/.54—dc23
LC record available at https://lccn.loc.gov/2020035410

For
Bennett

The notion came to me that everybody in the world was naked, in a way. . . . We were all sad, bare, forked creatures.

—Alice Munro, "Wenlock Edge"

The odds of not meeting in this life are so great that every meeting is like a miracle. It's a wonder that we don't make love to every single person we meet.

—Yoko Ono, liner notes for *Feeling the Space*

Contents

Sex with Strangers

Over Boy

Life hasn't much to offer except youth and I suppose for older people the love of youth in others.

F. Scott Fitzgerald, letter to his cousin Ceci

The cab dropped Keith at Campus, the club halfway between Harvard and MIT where students and their admirers congregated. At nineteen he'd been a regular, but for years now he'd disallowed himself the club, self-conscious of his tenure-track appearance. A shovel-faced bouncer demanded ID from skittish boys, and Keith recalled, from his precocious past, the terror of being carded and denied. Had that been less or more unsettling than his current fear, of not being carded? Mercifully, or mockingly, the bouncer asked for his license. Keith showed it and the doorman waved him through.

A more scrupulous bouncer would have noted that today was Keith's twenty-ninth birthday. This morning, shaving, he'd stared glumly into the bathroom mirror. His own reflection had once been a potent masturbation aid—the waifish torso, the glockenspiel abs—but now he was no longer his own type. His stomach wasn't fat but bereft of definition, as uninspiring as a sea without surf. Hair had begun to emigrate from the home shores of his scalp to the new worlds of neck and shoulder blades.

"Please," said LaWanda, his endoscopy assistant, when Keith griped about his failing looks. "You're not even thirty. You're just hitting your prime!"

"It's different when you're gay," Keith insisted. "It's like . . . it's like Olympic figure skating." (This was February 2002; the very next day, the Salt Lake Games would open.) "The stars," he said, "get younger and younger, and all of us former wunderkinds are forced to retire early."

Pleased with his quip, he repeated it at his birthday dinner party. Out of the dozen men around the table, just two chuckled.

"We don't *all* retire," said the horror-struck host, a burly, balding architect named Mitch. "Some of us turn pro."

Now everybody laughed.

For Keith's friends, the indignities of growing older seemed to be mitigated by the aging of their attractions. They might still appreciate the occasional college freshman in all his mint-condition glory, but the men they realistically sought and partnered with were graying and sagging just as they were.

Initially Keith had hoped that, just as his childhood yen for grape juice had yielded to cabernet, his sexual tastes, too, might mature. But his hope foundered on a lesson from medical school: the greater venturesomeness of an adult's palate was but a measure of how many taste buds had died. Keith didn't just happen to find youth beautiful. For him, who had been a young beauty, beauty *was* youth, and as he drifted farther from his own ideal, he felt doomed. If *he* couldn't find himself attractive anymore, how could he trust anyone else who claimed to?

It had been more than a year since he'd last had a boyfriend: Andy, a twenty-year-old concierge at the Park Plaza for whom pleasing others was as instinctual as swallowing. They'd shared four months of puppyish fun, but the day Andy found a gray hair on Keith's chest and plucked it with scientific curiosity, like an exotic orchid or heirloom fruit, Keith executed a swift, preemptive dump. Since then, not even a one-night stand (although there had been, in the Fens last summer, a dispiriting five-minute kneel). He tried the bars, but in his newly unconfident state, every word he spoke was inflected with doubt. He felt like someone who, after years of living abroad, returned home rusty at his own native tongue.

Which was why he should simply have gone to bed. Or accepted LaWanda's invitation for a nightcap. But he wanted to take advantage of this last birthday when, if he told people the occasion, and they asked how old he was, he could truthfully say a number starting with twenty.

~

Campus smelled like any club—cigarettes and sour, spilled beer—but layered within that was a more adolescent, locker-room musk of over-straining bodies. Keith checked his coat and readied for the plunge. He avoided the Eighties Room, where the tunes of his teenage years were served up with irony to kids who'd been singing "Old MacDonald" when the tracks were released. Instead he detoured to the lounge, where gaunt guys in ball caps flopped on couches. One, for some reason barefoot, dipped his toe in a cup of ice. Another blew a bubble of purple chewing gum, then pinched it off and passed it to a friend.

No one seemed to notice Keith but two thirtysomething men in matching blue tuxedos—what on earth? Standing against the wall with starched and benevolent expressions, they could have been chaperones at the senior prom, and they stared as if they knew something about him, something perhaps even he didn't know.

Escaping their gaze, he made his way toward the main dance floor, through that odd liminal zone of competing sound systems, like the salt point where a freshwater river gives way to sea, and then past it until he was drenched by repetitive house music. The recessed dance floor was surrounded by a railing at which the non-dancing spectators stood, looking variously predatory and afraid. Keith elbowed his way into a spot and tried to affect an expression that split the difference. There must have been a drink special, because all along the railing, cups filled with some periwinkle liquid glowed in the pulsing light like hokey, out-sized shamanic crystals. The comparison seemed apt to Keith, since everyone here, he suspected, including him, relied on a kind of primitive superstition. If I wear my lucky tank top, the boy-gods will smile on me. If I sip my drink *now*, he'll look back.

Beneath the clouds of disco smoke, guys danced with the fervency of a jungle tribe trying to conjure rain. Keith recognized one kid from the days he used to visit here, pre-Andy. The boy had a wide-eyed, just-slapped appearance and a long Pharaonic goatee. Keith recalled a previous night of watching the boy, of longing to soothe that ruddy, startled face, but when he looked closer and saw a snail-shaped birthmark beneath the boy's right ear, he realized it was someone else. The generations of club kids succeeded themselves as rapidly as lab mice.

He was budging toward the bar when a skinny shirtless boy pointed at him. The gesture seemed less flirtatious than accusatory. Was he being singled out as too old, an interloper? He pretended he hadn't seen, but again the boy pointed, so Keith touched his chest and mouthed, "Me?" The boy nodded.

Keith felt wooden and ludicrously conspicuous, as though it were he, not the couple in the other room, attired in formal wear, but he side-stepped out amid the throng, using dancers' slippery shoulders for hand-holds. A billowing thunderhead was released from the smoke machine and he stumbled with a blind man's halting gait.

When the smoke cleared, he was next to the boy, who looked at him with baby-seal eyes. His nose was eagerly upward-pointing, his blond hair stringy and dark with sweat. The boy stared at Keith's necklace—a generic silver chain—then touched it reverently, as if expecting it to emit heat or light. "Cool necklace!" he said.

"Thanks," said Keith. "I like"—he searched for a suitably reciprocal compliment—"your stomach."

But the kid had already rocketed away into another private orbit. Keith stood there, whiplashed with shame and disappointment.

Imagine driving to a distant store to use a coupon, only to find that the coupon has expired; you'd feel suckered to pay full price for the item but would want to buy something so the trip's not a total waste. Keith began to dance.

Like a pair of rusty scissors, his legs felt blunt and unproductive. His arms were out-of-sync metronomes. He didn't want to be seen searching for the boy, so he closed his eyes, pretending absorption in the music, and after a few awkward unbalanced seconds realized, pleasantly, that he was indeed absorbed, the bass beat an axis around which his body spun. He softened into the motion and the noise.

Then there was a touch on his throat and he opened his eyes to see the boy again, his finger back on Keith's necklace, tracing it, insistent, as though Keith had only imagined his earlier abandonment.

Tentatively, Keith ran his own index finger along the boy's and found his knuckle hairless, as smooth as sea glass. His chest, Keith saw, was hairless too, but for a sparse patch at his sternum that, like the proverbial fig leaf whose outline it resembled, only drew attention to what it should have hid: his youth.

Nineteen, Keith guessed. A sophomore.

"I'm Keith," he said, offering his hand.

The boy used the hand as leverage and pulled himself close enough to aim his breath into Keith's ear. "Ryan," he said, and kissed Keith on the neck.

It was a small triumph that filled Keith with disproportionate confidence. The local slang was coming back to him.

"Student?" he asked.

Ryan nodded. "Tufts. And you?"

Keith was grateful for the question's open-endedness, as if he, too, might still be a sophomore. "I work in a hospital," he said, using the vague formulation he'd devised as a less off-putting alternative to "gastroenterologist." Most people never pressed for details, perhaps surmising him a lab technician or insurance administrator.

"Cool," said Ryan with the same fixated enthusiasm he'd lavished on Keith's necklace. His gaze was like a needle stitching into Keith's. "Hospitals are so . . . big," he went on. "There's that weird lighting. Hey, do you swim?"

Keith was confused. "In the hospital?"

"Nah, I just thought your neck smelled like chlorine."

In fact, Keith had swum that morning, a half mile at the YMCA pool. "Yeah," he said. "Maybe I should have showered longer."

"I like it," Ryan said. "Makes me think of summer, the Good Humor man." He ran his thumbs along the bone of Keith's forehead. "Ooh, wow—you've got killer eyebrows!"

His burbling stream of consciousness began to drown Keith's self-doubt. Keith made his hand into a cup and mimed sipping. "Want a drink?"

Ryan grinned beatifically and said, "Rolling."

"Rolling Rock?"

"Nah, I'm rolling. I'm on X. Just water for me." He held up a clear plastic bottle in which an orange glow stick fluoresced.

"Gotcha," Keith said. So much for his native speaking.

Keith had never done Ecstasy. A decade back, when he'd started clubbing, his crowd had been mostly drinkers who dabbled with the sporadic line of coke. Then had come the long pleasure-denying hibernation of med school and residency, and when at last he'd blinkingly emerged and observed the new cult of group-hugging, love-professing ravers, he felt he'd missed a collective conversion.

His doubts, like those of most skeptics, veiled underlying jealousy. Could a pill make him, too, born again? But he feared that without a younger guide, any attempt to enter this new realm would be unseemly: a geezer at a G-rated cartoon. (He'd hoped at one point that Andy would lead the way, but Andy's youthful high was so naturally powerful that he'd had no need for synthetic help.)

Ryan offered Keith his glowing water, and Keith accepted, half expecting his throat to burn, but the liquid was soothing, analgesic.

"The music!" Ryan said.

"I know," said Keith, not sure if he had just confirmed the Tourettically redundant beat as good or bad. Then he realized that for Ryan right now, everything was good.

Ryan's pupils were huge, like portals into another dimension, and his smile, too, suggested a time traveler's bewildered thrill. He kissed Keith again, this time on the mouth, his breath smelling faintly of banana, then spun to bestow his attentions on someone else. Now Keith understood the kid's turning away not as selfishness but generosity. Ryan—at least the chemically aided Ryan—was a true philanthropist: a lover of all mankind!

And mankind, it was clear, returned the love. Ryan danced with bee-like industry, zooming from boy to boy to collect their fawning recognition. But every few minutes, he circled back to Keith.

"Owdy-hay, Eith-kay," Ryan greeted him after his latest circuit.

"Itto-day, Yan-ray," Keith said. He appreciated the music of the boy's name in pig Latin: like "ion ray," a high-tech seduction beam.

Ryan turned Keith around and rubbed his cool, clammy fingers on Keith's back, as in the game Keith had played long ago with his mother, when she traced letters on his skin and made him decipher the resulting secret message, except that Ryan seemed to shape only the letter *o*, again and again, as though trying to summon a genie from Keith's flesh.

Eventually, Ryan moved up to Keith's scalp, massaging expertly. "God, I love your hair," he said.

Keith sighed. "What's left of it."

Ryan whipped him around so they were facing, inches apart, his banana breath hot on Keith's lips. "Listen. I'm gay, right?—which means I'm attracted to *men*. What could be more manly than male-pattern baldness?" He pulled Keith's head down and tongued the path of his receding widow's peak.

Keith noticed people noticing them. The tuxedoed couple had appeared at the railing, blue drinks in hand to match their outfits. He couldn't tell if they looked at him with censoriousness or envy, and he realized, with a bracing free-fall tickle in his groin, that he didn't particularly care.

"Eith-Kay," Ryan asked, "how old are you?"

Keith didn't hesitate. "Twenty-nine. As of this morning."

"Oh my God, are you serious? Why didn't you say something?" Ryan leapt into the air, clapping his hands, then pogo-sticked manically through the crowd. "It's his birthday! It's his birthday!"

Strangers offered tipsy congratulations, glad for a new reason to celebrate.

"It's so weird," said Ryan, back at Keith's side. "Almost every guy I've ever dated has been either twenty-six or twenty-nine."

"I guess I met you just in time," said Keith.

"Plus, now I can give you a birthday present."

"Come on. That's silly. We just met."

"No, I want to. I do. Will you let me?"

Ryan looked at him with his big dilated eyes—wishing wells into which Keith could aim his fantasies. Keith shrugged. "Well, maybe something small."

"It *is* small. It's tiny! You're gonna love it."

Ryan dug into his pocket and came up with a mini Ziploc bag, no bigger than a postage stamp. "Happy happy," he said, and handed it to Keith.

The pill inside was the color and size of Tylenol. One side was scored with a line; the other bore the cartoonish outline of a fist, thumb pointing up.

"Thumbs-ups are awesome," Ryan said. "Like Mitsubishis, but not as speedy."

"I don't know," Keith said, returning the bag. "I've never done it."

Ryan gasped. "The first time's totally the best!"

He whirled about Keith like a tetherball in the schoolyard game, spiraling tight, then out, then back. Keith imagined that Ryan's style in bed might be equally schoolboyish, and that if he took the pill, he'd get the chance to find out.

He checked his watch. It was only 11:30. He'd arranged to have no patients until tomorrow afternoon.

He was about to say yes when he saw Ryan pinch open the bag, shake the pill onto his palm, and pop it into his mouth. Keith's hesitation, he realized, had caused the boy to renege. Once again his outmodedness—and youth's fickleness—were confirmed.

Then Ryan's mouth was on his, and they were kissing, and Ryan pressed the pill onto Keith's tongue.

"You'll see," he said when he pulled away. "Everything changes."

Keith could think of nothing to do but flash the thumbs-up sign. He swallowed.

~

Ryan said that the X might take thirty or forty minutes to kick in, and that Keith should try just to forget about it and relax. But Keith couldn't. There was so much to keep track of. Drink lots of water, Ryan warned; if you feel nauseous, try not to throw up—you might lose the pill; if your jaw grinds, chew gum to keep it loose. Keith felt silly accepting this remedial instruction. He danced on, his feet trippy with nervousness, smiling the tight smile of a gambler who's bet beyond his limit.

"How are you feeling?" Ryan asked after half an hour that seemed like two. And then again, ten minutes later, "Feeling anything?" His blissed-out face was a postcard from a distant paradise: *Weather's beautiful, wish you were here.*

Ryan's ministrations were entirely well intentioned, but Keith, who felt nothing other than a late-night stubbornness in his knees, found himself blistering with resentment. He didn't know whether to be angry at Ryan for giving him a dud pill or at himself for being somehow inadequate, his aging brain perhaps too ossified to assimilate the drug.

He thought of the time, a couple of years after college, when he'd gone to City Hall for a Gay Youth Pride dance. The multi-pierced boy at the door asked his age. "Flattered!" said Keith. "You're doubting that I'm legal?" The boy glowered. "No over-twenties allowed." As Keith, too stung to protest, had silently slunk away, the kid and his teenage buddies had snickered.

But hadn't Keith himself once been a snickerer? Hadn't he let men sidle up to him on the dance floor and crow over his drum-tight stomach, then ridiculed them as they slaved to bring him drinks? His exclusion now from Ryan's paradise must surely be comeuppance. He deserved this jealousy, this lack of joy.

And then he wasn't feeling that way.

He didn't notice when everything shifted, but at some point it occurred to him that he was no longer wondering if or when the drug would work, no longer questioning himself or his place here, and he thought that perhaps that's what ecstasy truly was: the absence of doubt.

The music's repetitiveness wasn't bothersome anymore but now provided an enveloping, amniotic security. It was the sound a rainbow would make if rainbows made sound. Ryan smiled at him, and Keith saw deep in his mouth the glint of a silver filling, and in that spark a new universe could have been big-banged.

"Have you come up yet?" Ryan asked.

Keith nodded—at least he thought he nodded; his body's movement was hard to distinguish from the overall swirl. "Yeah," he said. "Wow. I think I have."

Up was the perfect word for it, and not the hyper up of cocaine—nothing to do with superiority, with one person higher than another—

but a soaring elevation of everything and everyone together. The club was lit as in a dream—inscrutable fogginess punctuated by bursts of clarifying brightness—and in those moments of clarity, Keith saw the dancers around him and recognized their multifarious beauty. Some were beautiful in their bodies, some their faces, some their eyes. Others, like Chinese ideograms, denoted charm or delicacy or sexiness with not-quite-literal but perfectly right approximations.

He saw the couple in the matching tuxes—what a touching, avuncular pair!—and before he quite knew what he was doing had crossed the floor and was introducing himself, kissing each man's cheek. "It's my birthday," he said, "and I want everyone to have a good time. Are you having a good time?"

"Yes," said the taller, African American one, whose name was Gary. "We're celebrating, too. It's our anniversary."

"Really?"

Steve, the shorter, blond one, nodded. "We met right here. Ten years ago tonight."

"Oh my God," said Keith, "that's awesome. Come out and dance."

He took each man by the hand and towed them onto the dance floor, their formation like the bow of a human icebreaker, but there was nothing violent in their movement through the crowd; all was gentleness, bonhomie, beneficence. Keith introduced Gary and Steve to Ryan, and Ryan introduced them all to a threesome he'd befriended in Keith's brief absence, and the gang writhed together as one big pod.

Could this be his true vocation, Keith wondered? Not diagnosing intestinal maladies but facilitating camaraderie among men? He felt born to the task, a retriever pup plunging into its first pond. He complimented Steve's haircut, told Ryan's friend what a wonderful smile he had. He was attentive, doting, generous: the better Keith he'd always hoped to be.

Next thing he knew his shirt was being tugged out from his jeans.

"Come on," Ryan said. "Take it off."

It had been ages since Keith had gone shirtless in a club—six or seven years at least, the point when the grooves of his abdomen had begun, like silt-collecting streambeds, to fill with fleshy sediment. He expected himself to protest, but instead his arms lifted into the air and he let Ryan peel the shirt away.

"That's better," Ryan said, and although Keith hadn't been aware of any problem, he understood at once the necessity of this solution.

With the glee of a child plugging in a new toy, Ryan poked his finger into Keith's exposed navel; Gary and Steve each rubbed a muscle of his shoulders. Keith saw how keeping himself covered would have been presumptuous—who was he to dispute the beauty of creation? Yes, he thought, gazing down at his pooched-out belly and the soft pewter whorl of hair upon it, even he was beautiful.

~

He danced, and danced and danced, because it would have taken greater effort not to. That's what the drug did to him. Motion was now his default, as were happiness and compassion and the sense that skin was one of God's minor mistakes, that in fact humans were meant to live all within the same membrane, conjoined at the vital organs, Siamese.

Man after man kissed him, each tongue with a different taste that made his mind change colors. There was Ryan's—salty but fresh, oceanic—which rippled blue wavelets through his brain. Then, attached to the boy with the startled face, a green tongue: cool, arboreal. Kissing was like breathing now, easy and essential. He felt a rush of sensation and simultaneous deep calm. Was this what a hummingbird experienced, moving at top speed but staying in the same place? He traced the Möbius strip of his emotions: he was happy because everyone here liked him; everyone here liked him because he was happy.

There were fingers (whose? not Ryan's) down Keith's pants and they found something unembarrassedly limp—something miraculous in its tiny limpness!—as different from the usual plump fruit of sexual response as a raisin is from a grape, and likewise concentrated in sweetness, as though its very pliability allowed previously blocked nerve endings to the surface. The fingers tugged and gently tugged, steering Keith down a tunnel of pleasure that he felt could extend indefinitely without reaching the light of release.

Then there was a hand again on his back, circling, circling, calling forth the genie that Keith now realized was his own self, his all-powerful spirit, finally freed from its vessel of doubt. He turned, planning to take Ryan's gifted hand and kiss it, to thank him for showing Keith the way. But the hand, he saw as he spun about and grabbed it, belonged not to Ryan—who was locked in a lambada with some Irish-looking hunk—but to a man Keith hadn't noticed before.

The man's posture was the first thing that struck him: the stalwart uprightness of a lighthouse that has stood, by good design and no small measure of providence, the battering of countless gales. He had about him, too, something of a lighthouse's anachronistic elegance, his hair (the soft gray of weathered Cape Cod shingles) and his roughhewn, unpretentious jaw supporting a fantasy of simpler, better times: they don't make 'em like that anymore.

Keith guessed the man at fifty or fifty-five. There were kind crinkles around his mouth and at the corners of his heavy-lidded eyes, which Keith could tell, even in the club's erratic light, shone an energetic, vernal green. Keith remembered he was holding the man's hand. Instinctively, the way you clutch at an object tossed in your direction, he gripped the hand tighter and brought it to his mouth. He kissed each callused finger in succession.

"Charmed, I'm sure," said the man in a stately baritone that carried over the speakers' soaring anthem.

"More than charmed," said Keith. "My name's Keith."

"Stan," he said. "You didn't mind my being forward?"

"Life's short. Have to go for what you want."

As the words left him, Keith realized that what he wanted was to bury his face in Stan's chest. He didn't question the impulse, didn't think about Stan being nearly twice his age.

Through his barely damp T-shirt, Stan's chest was firm without being overly hard, more forgiving than the skin-and-bones rib cages Keith was used to. His sweat had the pleasantly musty, unhurried scent of the air in a favorite uncle's attic.

"What do you do, Keith?" he asked. "I mean, when you're not kissing strangers' hands in clubs?"

"I work in . . ." Keith began his standard evasion, but for once, braced by the drug and by Stan's solidness, he decided to be forthright. "I'm a doctor," he said. "Gastroenterologist."

Stan smiled, doubling the lines around his eyes. "I see, a plumber." He sounded neither dismissive nor particularly impressed. "My dad was a plumber. Houses, though, not people."

"Totally right!" Keith said. "Pipes and drains, same basic deal. How 'bout you?"

"Restoration. Tables, chairs—anything that can fit through a door, I fix it."

"Wow," said Keith. "That's awesome. That's *amazing*. I mean, saving things that might be thrown away? Salvation?"

The Ecstasy made everything a metaphor. Life was a poem, endlessly enjambing.

"Sorry," said Keith. "Am I gushing? I'm on Ecstasy."

"Aha," said Stan. "I thought you were being a little . . . friendly. Well," he added with mock schoolmarmishness, "kids today. What can you expect?"

"Me? I'm not a kid. I'm twenty-nine. It's my birthday. Or yesterday, before midnight. And I've never done it before. But this guy—he *is* a kid, really really cute—Ryan, he gave it to me, he's the blond one, skinny . . ."

Keith searched for Ryan, but he and the Irish dreamboat must have decamped to the lounge. This observation wasn't worrisome, it was merely new information—as though someone had repainted the scene's backdrop in a different, equally pleasing shade.

Stan anchored two firm hands on Keith's shoulders. "Listen. Keith. You said you didn't mind my being forward. It's five minutes to two. I live just down the road."

Stan's voice had an irresistible authority. He beckoned with the promise of comfort, like an old sofa with sags in all the right places.

"Do you want to come home?" he asked.

Keith wasn't sure he said yes, but he was operating in a new language, one without a word for no. And so they were retrieving their coats from the coat check, and sleeving into them, and approaching the door.

He paused near the exit to scan once more for Ryan. The kid wasn't there, or, if he was, Keith couldn't distinguish him among the crowd of glittering men. He felt the passing shadow of an emotion that he guessed under normal circumstances would be disappointment, but since disappointment did not exist for him just now, nor regret, he only smiled with the memory of Ryan's breath in his ear.

~

Stan said he lived in a loft in Cambridgeport, fifteen minutes' walk at most. They passed a pair of Indian restaurants, a hardware store, a fire station. The walking didn't bother Keith. It was like dancing but in a different key.

"Warm enough?" Stan asked.

Keith said, "Dandy." He had just been noticing how the cold crystallized his vision into prismatic shards. Each blink clicked the kaleidoscope to a new color scheme. But in his core, he was soupy with warmth.

Stan snugged his hand into Keith's back pocket. "Do you usually go home with older men?"

"I don't usually *leave* home in the first place," Keith said, and they both laughed a disburdening laugh. Keith was enough himself to realize that tricking with Stan broke all his normal rules, but perhaps, he thought, building your personality was like pumping up your muscles: you had to strain them so when they healed, they'd be stronger.

A downdraft nipped from an alleyway. It brought a smell Keith couldn't exactly place: fruity and pheromonic and verging on too sweet, with a sultry mulled undertone of clove.

"What is that?" he asked.

Stan pointed to the sign on the building they were passing: New England Confectionery Company. Keith noticed, on the roof, the building's water tower, painted in retro pastel stripes. "Necco wafers?" he said, incredulous.

"Maybe," said Stan, "but probably Sweethearts—those little candy valentines? In February, they bake around the clock."

Keith inhaled again. The now-familiar aroma made him nostalgic for his childhood and, foolishly, for an even earlier age, before he was born. It was the smell of gee whiz and backseat drive-in fumblings, the candied innocence of romance itself.

In minutes they were at Stan's building, a sprawling brick warehouse that housed a lamp factory and the packing facility for a jigsaw puzzle maker. Styrofoam peanuts were littered about the entry. They rode a clanking elevator to the fourth floor and stepped into the middle of a living room that seemed centered on the elevator itself, the way you might expect to find a room focused on a television. A love seat and couch, upholstered in blood-colored cloth, angled kitty-corner around the mechanism. The main source of light was a model of the human skeleton that had been hung from a ceiling beam and fitted with bulbs in the eye sockets.

"I think of the decor as kind of postmodern rummage sale," Stan said.

"It's great," said Keith. "And, God, all this space."

But the loft's lack of boundaries was off-kiltering. It stretched unfathomably, without proper walls. There was a bed in one area, a desk and bookcase in another; under a window, Keith saw a sink and stove.

He detected the whiff of paint remover and polyurethane, of objects being stripped and reborn. "Is this where you work, too?" he asked.

Stan gestured toward a corner curtained off by drop cloths. "I'll show you later, okay? In the morning."

Something about the change from outside to in had made Keith creaky and oversensitive, the way an ice cube cracks when dropped into a drink. He shivered and flapped his ashen hands.

"It's tough to heat," said Stan. "But I've got a few space heaters."

He stalked around the room, stooping periodically and flipping switches until a haunted humming filled the air. Keith removed his coat and soaked up the warmth.

Stan came from behind and engulfed him in a hug. "Have I told you how adorable you are?" He kissed Keith on the beginnings of his bald spot. "It's such a nice change to go to Campus and find someone cute but already a grownup. I mean, a doctor! My mother would be thrilled."

Keith hadn't thought of Stan as someone with a mother. "You're a nice change, too," he said. "You're so . . ." But he got stuck, and simply gripped Stan's arms.

Stan moved his hands down and patted Keith's stomach. "I know some guys would say I should just retire gracefully, or spend my time at one of those wrinkle bars. But I don't feel old. Isn't it about how you feel?"

Yes, Keith thought. Hadn't he recently had the very same insight? Or was that just something he'd read once in a book? His clarity was an ebbing tide.

"If you don't mind," said Stan, "I'm going to hop in the shower, wash the smoke out of my hair. Can I get you something? Orange juice? A beer?"

"I'm okay," said Keith.

"All right, then. Make yourself at home." He disappeared into the murk beyond the bed.

Keith mazed his way through the makeshift rooms, acclimatizing to the odd layout. His feet were still floaty, his vision slightly aswirl. The sawdusty air pricked at his skin. He found a stereo and CD cabinet: Lou Reed, Carly Simon, three versions of Handel's *Messiah*. There was jazz, too, and Keith picked a Miles Davis recording, *Kind of Blue*, because the cover was the color of his thoughts.

Returning to the apartment's center, he stared at the hanging skeleton lamp, which seemed an ill-conceived literalization of some cliché he couldn't quite recollect. The lamp swayed in imperceptible currents of air from the space heaters, sending bony shadows skittering about the floor.

He sank into the love seat, which from this proximity he saw was less the shade of blood than of rust. There was an end table between the love seat and the couch, and on it sat a glass bowl of candies. Necco Sweethearts—Stan no doubt kept them handy in honor of his neighbor.

Keith scooped a handful and read their quaint memos: BE MINE. I WONDER. IT'S TRUE. Others were more recent messages: EMAIL ME. GOT LOVE? AS IF. Keith rattled the candies like dice, then dismissed them back into the bowl. What if people actually conversed in these silly epigrams? Could you conduct an entire romance that way?

He fished for another batch and came up with a reddish heart—cherry? cinnamon?—with its motto inked in purple: OVER BOY. He read it again, confused. "Over boy"? The opposite of "it boy"? Then he studied the candy closer and found a faint impression of the initial *L* the machine had mis-stamped.

The absent letter, like a missing tread on the staircase of his thoughts, sent him tripping into memory: third grade. It was Valentine's Day, and to ensure that everybody received at least one card, each student had been assigned a secret sweetheart. Keith's was Lisa Crosby.

In class, he deposited his valentine ("For Lisa—true friendship, always") in the milk-crate "mailbox" Miss Kenton had constructed, and wondered whose private passions he would receive. After attendance, Miss Kenton upended the box. One by one, she summoned each recipient, reading the names with exaggerated titillation, as if, despite her rigged system, getting a valentine should be a big surprise. "Mandy Coughlin? Ooh, look, someone sent you one! And Daniel Glick—you got one, too!"

When Lisa's name was announced, Keith watched her read his note, filling with a hot hope that he had been her secret sweetheart, too. But soon Miss Kenton's pile of cards was gone, and Keith's name still had not been called. He wasn't Lisa's sweetheart. He wasn't anyone's.

"Happy Valentine's Day," the teacher said. "Aren't you all just lucky to be so admired?"

"But wait, I didn't get one," Keith said.

Miss Kenton's face clouded with distress. She shook her mailbox, checking in vain for a stranded card. "Well, then, you can be *my* sweetheart," she said, and she came over to Keith and hugged him too tightly. She smelled powdery. Her arms were empty bags.

Keith had sat there, a fist in his throat, squeezed by Miss Kenton's baggy arms and by the shame of being unwanted even when the odds were fixed.

~

"Good choice," said Stan, snapping his fingers to the jazz.

Keith furtively popped the OVER BOY heart into his mouth.

Stan was wrapped in a towel, his gray chest hair beaded with water. Wisps of steam rose from his scalp like muddled thoughts.

"Glad you found the stereo," he said. "I should've shown you. Hope I didn't take too long?"

"No, no, not at all," said Keith, and it was true, he couldn't fault Stan for anything—the man was generous and considerate and squarely handsome—and yet everything, Stan, the music, the apartment, was starting to feel wrong, or not really wrong but less than perfectly right, and Keith understood that the slow seep back of doubt, and the fact that his brain had allowed such a painful memory, meant the fading of his Ecstasy.

On his tongue, the candy heart was dissolving to a sludge, its taste not as sweet as the factory fumes but chalky and bitter, medicinal. Stan approached him, smiling, and embraced him in his damp arms. Keith felt the knot of Stan's towel pushing into him, and below that, something equally hard, also pushing.

He pulled back for a moment, hoping to overcome his qualms. He tried to look at Stan the way Stan must look at a piece of furniture, beneath the chipping varnish and grimy surface dings to the striking heartwood original. And Keith sensed that he could—he could see Stan's inner grace, or he could learn to. What he wasn't sure he could see again was his own.

Stan kissed him, determinedly, the grizzle of his chin scraping Keith's. Keith kissed back as best as he could. He pressed what was left of the Sweetheart onto Stan's tongue, wishing it were a pill like the one Ryan had given him, and that he could grant that magic to Stan, and to himself.

You Are Here

Given a clear day, Father Tim was hoping to move confession to the Liberty Deck, where penitents could come clean beneath the pure tropical sun. But this Monday, as on the first two days of the *Destiny*'s voyage, the sky is a sallow mess of cloud, and by lunchtime there's unrelenting drizzle. After the meal, he heads for the chaplain's office, a revamped supply room by the Pirate's Cove Casino.

A short, fiftyish woman waits already by the door. Her hair is limp and lusterless—what his mother, who grew up in Wisconsin, would call "sauerkraut hair." But her mouth, precisely lipsticked, looks expectant, even brave. "Pardon me," she says. "Are you the priest?"

For the cruise, Father Tim has ditched his collar, identifying himself only by a blue name tag that says FATHER TIM in cheery sans-serif type and that, he now notices, is camouflaged against his azure guayabera. He points to the tag. "Truth in advertising."

Her gaze follows his finger, then darts back to his face, then takes in the whole of him again. He can tell she expects a priest to be older than twenty-seven, with a puffy, underwhelming body and burst-capillary nose, not his firmly gym-enhanced physique. The sunglasses probably don't help, either. He removes them and says, "Step into my office."

The *Destiny Daily* lists today's office hour as "confession," but given the holiday atmosphere, and because it's his twentysomething style, there will be no "Bless me Father, for I have sinned." It's his very first time hearing confession; only just last month was he was ordained. In this floating village where every imaginable service has been arranged, Father Tim is the hired shoulder to cry on.

The lipsticked woman, it seems, has gotten a jump start on the crying. The skin below her eyes looks like dough that's risen and been punched down. She sits in one of two canvas director's chairs—coral-and-white, the *Destiny*'s official colors—and Father Tim takes the other. Aside from the chairs, all that's provided in this makeshift confessional is an end table and a box of Kleenex. The space is sharp with the smell of deodorizer.

The woman crosses and recrosses her arms. "I'm bad," she says, and he's about to reassure her that despite our mistakes, we are all created in God's image, when he realizes what she said was "I'm Babs."

"Welcome, Babs. How's the cruise? You here on your own or with someone?"

"My husband, Les," she says. "It's our twenty-fifth anniversary. The Renewal of Vows package."

"Aha! You know I'll be officiating at the ceremony on Friday."

Babs picks at her carefully painted fuchsia fingernails, on each of which a glitter star's been glued.

"The Renewal of Vows," says Father Tim, treading conversational water. "They spoiling you rotten?" Through the thin wall between them and the casino, he hears the crisp click of poker chips.

"Oh, it's just perfect," she says in a scraped-thin voice. "It's all just too perfect. His-and-hers bathrobes, fresh orchids every morning. Today, breakfast in bed—took one bite and threw up."

"You're having trouble with Les?" he surmises.

A single tear forms at the lip of Babs's eyelid. He plucks a Kleenex, presses it into her hand.

"It's all right," he says. "We all hit rough patches." But what does he know of marital woes? He's never had his own—and now, of course, never will.

Les, she says, is a good man, a solid, loving dad. Crop insurance salesman—they live in Great Bend, Kansas—specializing in hail and twister damage. So what if he's no Tom Cruise? His Bud belly, his droopy ears: she's fond of them, the way you come to cherish an old farmhouse, its pantry not quite level with the kitchen. "But I've never felt, you know"—she downshifts to a whisper—"the way you're really supposed to. *That* way."

That way, thinks Father Tim. How do any of us know how "supposed to" feels? For years, he worried the faith he felt—the steadiness he called faith—failed some test of righteousness.

Babs's tears are flowing now. He lays the box of tissues in her lap.

"Something's always been missing," she says, "but I wouldn't let myself see what. The kids kept me busy. Now they're gone, Jenna to K-State and last year Kyle to Notre Dame, and the empty feeling's back, even worse—like, no matter where I go, what's really happening is happening somewhere else."

He wants to pat her shoulder, but these days, you can't be too careful about boundaries. He's been trained, whenever it's one-on-one, not to touch.

"All this new free time," says Babs. "What was I gonna do? Started surfing the web a lot, fooling around on Facebook. Do you know FarmVille? That's how I met Denise."

The rest pours out in hot, hushed, rapturous shame. Denise is from Salina. A social worker, sandy-haired and tall. They've gotten together a dozen times, when Les was checking crops. They've talked and hugged. Kissed, but nothing more.

Father Tim is staggered. He'd seen Babs as a dead stump, and missed the dogged, greening force inside.

"With her," says Babs, "I feel I'm finally *there*. Know what I mean? We're the center. Everything else dissolves."

Can he condemn her thrill in a change he, too, has felt? She's just described—better than he's ever managed to—the centripetal force of opening himself to God, when suddenly he started living at life's hub. But what he fell in love with is the source of love itself ("We love Him because He first loved us"); Babs loves . . . a woman from Salina? He stares hard and asks, "Does Les know?"

"Suspects something, but he'd never guess what." Her hair has fallen across her eyes, like shocks of wheat battered by a squall. "It's wrong," she says. "I know it's wrong."

Does she want him to absolve her or to say, *Yes, it's a sin, you have to stop*?

"Marriage is a sacred commitment," he begins. "A commitment to Les and to God." It comes out tinny, first notes from a borrowed instrument. "But you also have a commitment to yourself. How can you honor God's truth if your own life is false?" That's closer, almost his normal voice. "The key," he says, "is telling between what *feels* true and what *is*."

A cheer comes from the casino, and then a muted jackpot clang—someone else's luck. Father Tim looks into Babs's runny eyes and sees in them, blurry and reduced, himself. "Renewing your vows," he says. "You feel that would be false?"

"I feel," she says, "like jumping overboard."

~

After she's gone, Father Tim waits out the rest of the hour. He wants to keep the door open so other visitors will know he's available, but like all doors on the *Destiny*, this one shuts itself with coffin-lid finality. He pulls his chair to the threshold and makes himself a human doorstop.

What else could he have done for Babs—told her to pray, to recite the rosary? All he gave her was another minute of butterfingered advice and an offer to meet again, any time.

Ukuleles tinkle from a lower deck, the kind of music that might accompany a limbo contest. (On this ship, it probably does.) A month ago, at the Catholic Games, the tongue-in-cheek seminary Olympiad, he placed second in the Don't-Get-Stuck-in-Limbo competition. How he misses St. Thomas already: the brotherhood of seekingness; the holy, joyful striving. That was nothing more than preparation for this, now: the chance to tend a flock. But what if it turns out he enjoyed the long rehearsal better than the actual performance?

The hour passes without another caller. People take cruises, he thinks, to indulge in fresh sins, not generally to reconcile old ones. He replaces his chair, debating whether to head straight to his cabin or to hit the spa for some thalassotherapy.

The door slams behind him, and his still-full stomach lurches as though a wave has broadsided the ship. He's steadying himself when someone calls his name.

"Tim?" she says again. "It *is* you!"

He turns to face a woman in a *Destiny* uniform, eyes hidden by mirrored aviators. Her skin is tanned to the hue of his crème brûlée from lunch.

"Don't you recognize me?" She whips off the sunglasses, frees her hair from a coral baseball cap.

When he sees all of her, his gut lurches again. "Alison," he says. "Can't believe it." She's beautiful as ever: catlike, all arches and grace. But gone is the undergrad's lookaway expression, replaced by a disarming, full-bore stare.

"It's so good," he says, forgetting to add "to see you." "Are you here for . . ." He gestures to the supply room / chaplain's office. "Something you want to confess?"

She looks at him perplexedly, then at the door, then back at him. "You aren't? Oh my gosh, you *are*." She taps his name tag and hoots. "Father Tim! No, Father, I have nothing to confess. I mean, other than what you already know."

"Then what are you—"

She points at her uniform. "Shore excursion manager. But right now, I'm on my way to the goombay drumming show. Come on, it'll be a blast."

She tugs him toward the Paradise Lounge.

~

What'll I wear? was the first thing Tim wondered when he opened his last semester's grades. The seminary had a deal with Sun Line Cruises, filling one slot each year in the chaplaincy rotation. The junket went to the graduate with the highest marks in his class; Tim's final cluster of A's clinched it.

He knew the week at sea wouldn't be a free ride. But he thought of *Love Boat* reruns he used to watch with his mom, in which kindly Doc, the shipboard physician, dispensed Band-Aids and an occasional aspirin but mostly socialized and lived the good life. Tim imagined himself on the *Destiny* as a similarly carefree doctor of the soul, applying spiritual Mercurochrome: *Say two Hail Marys and meet me at shuffleboard.*

Comparing himself to a TV personality wasn't especially far-fetched; strangers did it to him all the time. "That guy from CNN?" they'd guess, stopping him on the street; or, in line at Dunkin', tapping him on the shoulder, "Weren't you in that thing with Morgan Freeman?" He had a best-supporting-actor sort of handsomeness, softened by just enough imperfection that people felt they could approach him but that doing so was a privilege. The dimple between his eyebrows gave him an affect of compassionate concern. A chronic crick tilted his neck unconsciously to the left, so he always seemed to be listening for trouble.

Already in his role as a deacon, Tim had seen how good looks worked to his advantage. Other seminarians, with their frail figures and acne-scarred chins, gave off a eunuchy air of hopelessness; people pitied them, discounted their advice. But Tim's fair eyes and veiny forearms won the interest of even the most agnostic parishioners. If the church's message was gripping enough to win this genuine hunk, maybe they, too, should listen up.

His turn to the church was unexpected. He'd always called himself a Catholic because his father had been one, and that trumped his mother's lapsed Lutheranism, despite—or perhaps because of—his father having absconded when Tim was six. But without his father to impart its rituals, Tim's Catholicism lived in him as a palpable absence, like the whiff of incense that haunts a room after the stick is snuffed.

At eighteen he chose Boston College, not for its Jesuit tradition but because they offered the best scholarship. He enrolled in the School of Management, intending to manage his way into the middle class. He was not ashamed of his family's poverty, but it wearied him. Almost every night of his childhood, he'd been woken at 1:00 a.m. by his mother's return from moonlighting at the diner; her car door's slam was the very sound of her prospects closing off. She'd been caught unprepared when her husband walked away, too reliant on her faith in love alone.

Tim breezed through his first semester, acing Statistics and Intro to Accounting, although the courses, like most everything, bored him. He liked his classmates, or at least wanted to be liked by them, investing in their attention as if buying futures in social standing. He was asked to pose for the "Men of BC" calendar, and he agreed because the photographer let him keep the varsity wardrobe. He strode across campus with ground-gulping strides, dressed as the man he thought he longed to be.

In his second year, he met Alison, star shortstop of BC's softball team. She was pixyish and lean and looked finely bruiseable, but there was infield dirt beneath her fingernails. He got a kick from her alertness, the way she charged into conversations as if each comment were a grounder to be scooped. Their sex was all hustle, headfirst.

For spring break, Alison joined an immersion service project: ten days at an El Salvador orphanage. Tim signed up, too, wanting to prove himself worthy of her affections. Maybe her faith in him would boost his faith in himself.

The orphanage director was Padre José, a priest who, with his unflinching stare and hydrant-thick neck, would have made a convincing fireman. In fervent English, he talked about his mission: The orphanage was a construction site, where boys learned to frame walls, tape Sheetrock, shingle roofs; as they were building their own dwellings, he built them into men. As orphans, they were lacking in emotional infrastructure, but he would teach them love from the ground up. "Who was Jesus? A carpenter!" he preached.

Afterward, Alison wanted to explore the town's cafés, but Tim said he would look for her later. He stayed up past midnight with the fire-eyed priest, sharing philosophy and sharp homemade rum.

In the morning, they excavated a new foundation hole for an addition to house the youngest boys. Tim's palms blistered, a satisfying pain. When the shovel hit a rock, it hummed like a tuning fork, and his whole body, too, reverberated. With every shovelful he moved, he felt his own hollowness filling up.

That Sunday, in Padre José's whitewashed church, Tim received his first Communion in years. Then, during the prayer of peace, he gripped the clay-caked fingers of two orphans—an even deeper comfort than holding hands with Alison. An anchoring. He felt unshakable.

Back at school, he went to Mass. Every week, at first, then every day. BC's Gothic towers and its golden eagle bust—emblems of all he'd wanted to achieve—now seemed flimsy backdrops to a much more urgent drama. He had always been skeptical of see-the-light accounts. This wasn't like that, he assured himself—but it almost was. No sparkling revelation, no bolts from on high, but an unforeseen inevitability.

Before, he had felt like a river's fickle current; now he felt like the riverbed. He woke each day with a trembling heart, as if in love.

It was softball season. Alison had on her game face when he tried to explain himself. They stopped assuming they would spend weekends together. The spare toothbrush in his bathroom went unused. On Easter Monday, through his soft tears and Alison's barbed silence, Tim officially broke things off.

In May, during finals, he got an email. "I've been thinking of you," wrote Padre José. "That look in your eyes when you hugged the boys good-bye. You have so much more to give. Will you let yourself?"

Tim withdrew from the School of Management and transferred to St. Thomas. His classmates couldn't fathom the switch. Did he realize the income he'd forego? But money—like romance, like a father—could disappear. The need to serve, and the loving God who made him yearn to serve: no matter what, they would always be there.

The day he moved, he saw Alison at the campus bookstore, trading in a stack of used texts. She was dating the ace on the baseball team, she boasted. Her smile was so tight it must have hurt.

~

Father Tim scans the Jolly Roger Room. He's four minutes early for their meetup. This afternoon, just as they were settling in for the goombay drumming show, Alison was summoned by her office—some problem scheduling a parasailing trip. She proposed this late-night drink as a rain date.

The Jolly Roger Room is where, in the morning, Father Tim celebrates Mass. At that hour, with its velveteen hush and redolent dimness, it's not altogether unchurchly; crowded now with boozers, it strikes him, decor-wise, as "watered-down bordello."

On a table just inside the entry sits a twice-life-sized bust of a woman. Oddly jaundiced, the sculpture looks familiar. He's puzzling over the resemblance when a thin, goateed man presents himself. Visitors to the Jolly Roger Room, he explains, have their photos taken and dumped into a bowl; each day he plucks one out and carves a corresponding "Butter Bust."

Catchy, Father Tim acknowledges—he saw something similar at the Wisconsin State Fair—but he tells the man no thanks, not for him.

"You must!" the artist insists, aiming a Polaroid before he can duck away.

At the front of the lounge, bathed in black light that makes their teeth fluoresce, Kip's Kalypso Kings libidinously perform. Kip, a jowly, ash-skinned man who, according to his bio on the drinks menu, once sang backup for Jimmy Buffett, croons "Day-O" as if it were a love song. Father Tim decides to walk the deck a minute, hoping Alison will be here when he returns. As he pivots, a tap on his waist halts him.

"*Hey, Father,*" says Alison. Her tone is cozy, suggestive, the same way she used to say "Hey, Twinkle"—to which his frisky reply would be "Hey, Star."

But now he just jokes, "Hi, come here often?"

She leads him to a booth. Where she touched his waist, he feels a phantom grip.

Alison orders a strawberry margarita. When Father Tim asks for Glenlivet on the rocks, she arches an eyebrow.

"What'd you expect?" he says. "A Virgin Mary?"

"I'm just surprised you'd spring for the good stuff. You were always a well-drink kind of guy."

He likes how they've slipped back to their old repartee. It's all the more enjoyable now for being safer, their boundaries defined, so that neither one is trying to gain advantage. "You look wonderful," he says. "Really great."

"You're the one who's buffed and polished." She squeezes his biceps. "'Father What-a-Waste.' That's what my mom always called guys like you. Who'd have guessed that Mr. Men of BC Calendar would wind up a priest?"

"That was a long time ago," he says.

Alison plays with the parasol that came with her margarita, the same magenta as her fingernails.

She never used to paint her nails, he thinks. "Tell me," he says, "how'd you end up here?"

She fills him in on the missing years: a softball-coaching stint at a prep school in Rhode Island, then back to Boston, a corporate PR firm. "A 'real' job, right? Put the communications degree to work. Communication? Ha. Ended up being me, alone at a desk, sending bullshit emails into the void." She swigs an antidote of margarita. "I'd always wanted to take a cruise, so when I quit, it's the first thing I did. I liked it so much, I made them hire me! Oh, don't look so shocked. Not like *you* never had a quick conversion."

The Jolly Roger Room has filled to capacity. At the next table, a trim black man and a grave-eyed Japanese woman sip from a scorpion bowl with Crazy Straws. Behind them sit an older, lei-wearing white couple, feeding each other calamari. The Kalypso Kings warble "I Want to Hold Your Hand." The couples moon at each other, swaying along.

The space between Father Tim and Alison seems to shrink and swell, like a balloon in fluctuating air pressure. It's been months since he's talked so close to a woman, outside of church.

"What about you?" she asks. "When you transferred, I was sure it was just a phase."

He shrugs. "It's a pretty long 'phase.'"

She twirls her mini parasol, then sucks its wet stem. "Was I that bad in bed? To make you swear it off for good?"

"The celibacy!" he complains. "Always the celibacy. Why is everyone so obsessed with that?" Then, seeing her chastened face, he softens. "But no, not any fault of yours. Trust me." In fact, he thinks often of her take-charge hands and tongue, the avid, expert shimmy of her hips. And more than that, her breakneck energy. In these cloistered years, he's clung to certain images: Alison head-sliding into home to beat a throw, a crescent moon of her lower back exposed; in El Salvador, Alison wolfing down an empanada, fresh salsa dribbling on her chin.

She takes his fingertips, a slight but ardent touch. "Can you try to explain? Why did you do it?"

How do you explain why even the blind know how to smile? Why whistling and laughter are contagious? "I know it looked sudden," he says. "But I'd always felt sort of . . . off course? Like I'd been reading the map upside down? After that service project, it was like someone finally turned it around, and boom, there was that arrow: YOU ARE HERE. The church is where I am. God is where."

She rubs his thumb. "I believe in God, too."

"But I want to *serve* Him. To make a difference. To help folks feel the groundedness I feel." He pictures Babs's earnest, stricken face.

"Can't you do that without," she says, ". . . you know?"

He yanks his hand away. "Still stuck on sex."

"No, it's just . . . okay, maybe I am. How can you pretend you don't feel it?"

"I do," he said. "Everybody does. That doesn't mean I have to express it genitally." He cringes at how clinical that sounds, tries again: "Ally, we're all of us finite. Choosing one thing means we have to give up something else."

"But aren't you scared of being lonely?"

He braces himself with a sip of scotch. "Most people get married for the wrong reasons," he says, parroting something his rector once told him. "Or incomplete reasons. Naive ones. But eventually they grow into it, and it's right. Maybe choosing celibacy is the same."

They sit at a silent impasse. When the waitress comes, they decline a second round. The neighboring couple—the black man and his somber-gazed companion—punch and slap at each other's shoulders. It's a mock argument, a tipsy mating display, but Father Tim senses genuine tension.

"The funny thing," says Alison. She twists her swizzle stick into a helix. "I kind of thought you and I would get married."

"Ally, we dated less than a year."

"I know, but I just had a feeling. Nobody else ever seemed so right."

A hot burst in his chest is both soothing and unsettling. He's swallowed too much scotch, or not enough. "Whatever happened to what's-his-name, with the curveball?"

"Topher? Uck, was that a bad rebound! The guy kissed like he was spitting chew."

They laugh at Topher's expense, and Father Tim is startled to feel how pleased he is by Alison's unkind words.

~

In the morning, it's back to the Jolly Roger Room for Mass. A dozen cruisegoers have showed up. There's a couple in matching canary jogging suits who bicker about the husband's need for a shave. Next to them, a raisin-faced, rusty-haired grandma minds her grandson, a sullen teen in board shorts.

Wearing full vestments in front of these vacationers, Father Tim feels risibly overdressed, a tuxedoed judge at a swimsuit competition. Earlier, he found the previous chaplain's note: "If you get too hot, the AC control's behind the bar—chasubles weren't designed for the tropics!"

Halfway through his homily something shifts, a change more of subtraction than addition, as when a blaring car alarm finally quits. He sees the effect on the worshippers' faces: they slacken with a kind of exalted relief. He'd like to think they're transformed by his words, or by the comfort of the Holy Spirit, but what they feel is that the *Destiny* has docked.

Thankful himself to be at this solid mooring, he ministers Communion to the bickering couple, to the grandma with the tarnished hair. He's placing the Host on the palm of her yawning grandson when he sees Babs at the back of the room. She slinks in, accompanied by a man with a corn-stubble crew cut and a cobblestone of a jaw. Father Tim beckons them, but they hang back, eyes trained down, as if respecting the privacy of someone scantily clad.

Only when Mass is done do they approach. Babs says, "Sorry we missed it. This is my husband, Les."

She looks better than before, her eyes less tear-inflamed, but in her voice, he still hears the heartache.

Les's handshake is surprisingly mealy for a man his size. "My fault," he says. "Hate to be late. But I couldn't for the life of me find my sunglasses. Babs says I've got Sometimer's disease—like Alzheimer's but less predictable. Ha ha!" He laughs as if reading aloud from a cartoon bubble.

"Funny thing," says Babs, "the Sometimer's almost always hits just as we're headin' to church."

"Oh, now," says Les. He pets her hand with habitual tenderness. "You going ashore today, Father?"

"Hadn't planned to," he says, slipping off his stole.

"Come with us. I predict it'll clear up this afternoon."

"I don't know," says Father Tim. Alison said Ocho Rios is her favorite port of call, but he's been thinking he'll stay onboard, maybe work out in the Buried Treasure Gym. He's found it hard to partake of the ship's relentless luxury and spends most of the time alone in his cabin, reading. He can see himself turning into his mother, who always orders the cheapest dish on the menu, even when she's being treated, because if she doesn't get used to pampering, then she can never miss it.

"Oh, come on," says Babs, "you can't skip Ocho Rios!"

"They've got it all planned out," Les adds. "A tour of some plantation thingy. A fish-fry lunch, maybe?"

He's not the world's most convincing pitchman. Father Tim wonders how much insurance he sells. But he thinks of Alison's enthusiasm, the giddy way she enunciated "shore excursion manager."

~

Alison stands at the gangway, clipboard in hand. Her tan is such a contrast to her uniform whites that she looks like a colorized image. Last night, in the lounge, Father Tim could smell her papaya hair conditioner; his nose fills now with the same cut-open scent.

"Too late to sign up?" he asks.

"For you? I think we can find a slot."

"Great! I've got my tacky shirt, my fancy old-school camera, my fat wallet: the ugly American."

"Yes, I see. Whatever happened to the vow of poverty?"

"Doesn't apply to parish priests," he says. He moves even closer to her. "So . . . you ready to *manage* my *excursion*?"

"You betcha. I'm going to manage you right on over to . . . Andrew." She points to a redheaded, Canadian Mountie–looking fellow. "He'll be leading your group to shore."

"You're not coming?"

"Way too high on the ladder now. I hold down the fort."

Father Tim's camera strap cuts into his neck. The sunscreen on his brow has gone gummy. He's thinking he should bag this when a hand lands on his shoulder.

"Fun and sun, here we come," says Les. Beside him stands Babs, her eyes red again.

Andrew, the rangy tour guide, blows a whistle.

"Guess we're out of here," Father Tim says to Alison. "Maybe we can find time later. Dinner?"

"Sorry," she says. "I'm booked."

"Okay, then, tomorrow?"

"I've got an evening staff meeting, but how about a nightcap? Same time and channel as before?"

"Sure," he says. "Sure. It's a date."

~

At the pier, a gold-toothed man, his face tiny within a tangle of dreadlocks, tunefully hawks Rasta caps and painted balsa carvings. Andrew warned of these often shady "higglers," so Father Tim marches on, ignoring the man's patter ("Mahogany! Black coral! Batik!"). But Les, seemingly enamored of the higgler's high-rent smile, stops to accept his soul-brother handshake.

"Come on," calls Babs. "We'll be late for the tour."

Les considers a tortoiseshell comb. "Nice? Maybe to bring back for Jenna?"

"Les, that stuff's illegal," says Babs. "Protected species, that's what Andrew told us. Didn't he, Father?"

Trying to stay neutral, all he says is, "Might be a risk at customs."

The Rastafarian hides the comb back in his bag, then fingers Babs's sauerkraut locks. "How 'bout da woman's hair—she wan' mi braid it?"

Les claps his hands. "Fun! Like a real Jamaican."

"No," Babs says, ducking away.

"Oh, come on, hon. Live a little."

"No!" she repeats and storms away, leaving the men to chase her.

"Don't know what's gotten into her," says Les. He sticks a pinkie into his ear and wiggles it as if trying to pick the lock of his own thoughts. "You suppose it could be the change of life?"

Seeing Les's lunkish expression, Father Tim feels helpless—it's like watching a sparrow hurtle into plate glass. How could two people live together for a quarter century and still know so little about each other? "Have you tried talking to her?" he suggests.

"She's not much of one for talking. She'd rather sit alone, fooling on her laptop."

Father Tim looks ahead to Babs's trudging form—her broad bottom in lime Bermuda shorts—and tries to imagine her with Denise. "I'd be happy to do what I can," he offers.

Les waves him off. "We'll work it out. Always have. That's why we're married."

They catch Babs and reconnoiter with the cruise ship group. Andrew—who, despite his aggressive chipperness, turns out to lead tours only to fund his PhD in criminal psychology—brings them to Good Hope Plantation. They learn about the life cycle of the banana plant, the proper way to carry a load of coconuts in a head basket.

Then it's on to a nearby waterfall—popular, Andrew informs them, as a marriage-proposal spot. This prompts a round of storytelling, as each couple recounts where they popped the question. Two newlyweds, by the sound of them Brooklynites, describe the thrill of saying yes on the Coney Island Cyclone, just as the roller coaster plunged. The pair from this morning's Mass, in the canary jogging suits, quibble over the site of their engagement: "Depends," says the man. "First or second time?" Babs and Les don't volunteer their story, but Father Tim watches a shadow of memory pass between them.

Over the waterfall's noise—its surging, ceaseless *yes*—he hears the Brooklyn wife calling out: ". . . favor . . . just married . . . would you mind?" She hands him an iPhone.

"My pleasure," he says. "There, against the falls?"

They pose in the self-evident spot, by a mist-brightened, heart-shaped outcropping, and Father Tim captures the shot. It's an image that must reside in a thousand honeymoon albums. But isn't that its point? At last you've joined the married club. You're in.

"Us next?" says the man from the jogging-suit couple. He foists another phone on Father Tim, who takes the shot.

Everyone turns to the last pair, Babs and Les. Babs ignores them and crouches down, dunking her hands as if she'd like to drown them.

Respectfully, the others avert their eyes. But Les, belly jiggling, hams it up. "My wife," he bellows, "is part Cherokee, her father's mother's side. Scared a picture's gonna steal her soul." He brandishes his Nikon—no "smart-ass-phone" for him, he's said—pretending it's a savage growling beast.

Babs glares. "I'm no such thing," she says.

"Oh yeah? If you're not Indian, what are you then?"

She dries her hands on her shorts. "Nothing. And you know it."

"Not to me," says Les. "You're everything. You're mine."

Babs startles, then shyly blinks. "Oh, quit fussing and get your dumb old shot."

Father Tim accepts the camera from Les and snaps a photo, then quickly snaps another, just in case.

The Brooklyn husband jokes that if church life gets too slow, the priest could always go into business. "A sideline," he says. "'Heavenly Photos.'"

Father Tim's own camera remains around his neck. None of them has offered to take his picture.

Lunch is at a grubbily charming corrugated-tin shack back in town. They're fed goat stew, fried dolphin, and salt-cod pancakes the cook calls "stamp-and-go." Everyone guzzles Ting, a local grapefruit soda that Father Tim decides, as it trills down his throat, achieves a kind of gustatory onomatopoeia.

He remembers something he's meant to tell Alison: a Salvadoran lunch shop he found in East Boston, where the *pupusas* are 100 percent authentic. He'd love to take her there, for old time's sake. He's forgotten to ask where she's based when the *Destiny* isn't sailing. Could she come to Boston? Where would she stay?

Just as dessert is served, the clouds that have dogged the entire voyage peel away, like bandages stripped to bare renewed skin. Andrew announces that the group will split up for the afternoon. There are glass-bottom-boat trips, catamarans, horseback tours. Be back on ship by five o'clock, he warns.

Father Tim approaches Babs and Les. Since the photo op, husband and wife haven't said much to each other, but their quiet now seems happily intimate. Les has a boat-shaped piece of papaya, Babs a plate of sliced sweetsop. They trade bites of their juice-dripping fruit.

"Father!" says Les. "Hey, how 'bout that sun? Did I tell you?"

"Sure did. I thought some snorkeling might be in order, to celebrate."

"Sounds fun," says Les. "But we already settled on one of those paddle boats. Take a couple of Red Stripes and drift around the bay."

"Yeah, absolutely. That could work, too."

The spouses exchange a low-lidded glance. "The boats only have two seats," says Babs.

"Of course," says Father Tim. "I wasn't thinking."

By now the others have all gone, so he makes his way alone to the beach. Lovers splash in the surf, and kids play at the shore, shaping sandcastle domes with coconuts. The sun stings like the aftermath of a slap.

~

The next day, they dock at Grand Cayman. Father Tim worries Les might propose another excursion, but thankfully he and Babs don't come to Mass. He wonders what this bodes for their marriage; they could be sleeping late together, or not speaking again.

Returning to his cabin, he takes a longcut past the gangway. Alison is snared in an argument with a man who insists his travel agent touted Grand Cayman's Mayan ruins.

"Could she have said Tulum?" Alison suggests. "Near Cozumel?"

"No! It's Cayman. She definitely said Grand Cayman."

Father Tim flashes a sympathetic smile, but she misses it.

He spends the morning secluded in his cabin. Sprawled in bed with his Kindle, he tries to lose himself in *Wise Blood*. After reading the same page three times, he gives up, his concentration shot by the awareness of all the reputed fun he's missing. He could be tracing figure eights at the ice-skating rink or sinking putts on the nine-hole green. There's the skydiving simulator, the Virtual Reality Center with its "motion-based undersea theme rides." If he were home, it would be the height of decadence to read Flannery O'Connor in bed, but in this temple of pleasure, where even the deck swabbers seem ecstatic in their work, anything less than the time of his life feels like failure.

At noon, he finally rouses himself for a stroll. For the first time in days, he's feeling queasy, so he sticks a motion-sickness patch behind his ear. The nausea confounds him: the ship is moored; the weather has calmed. Maybe it was the stamp-and-go.

He ascends to the Liberty Deck, where the sun, as if pissed off by days of passengers' griping, blazes with be-careful-what-you-ask-for. Given the browbeating heat, and with so many folks ashore, the deck is eerily deserted. Facing the sea, rows of empty pool chairs look like tombstones.

His stomach flares and clenches, not with nausea but with solitude—even worse than yesterday at the beach. *Aren't you scared?* asked Alison. *How can you pretend?*

Sure, he's fought pangs of desire, but hasn't everyone? Even married couples? His longings, during his tenure at St. Thomas, felt less urgent, the potholes in his chosen walk patched by camaraderie. Among impassioned peers, praying together three times a day, he could almost forget about the life-without-a-soulmate he'd signed up for.

"The 'discipline of celibacy,'" the rector often reminded them, "is not meant as an act of self-denial." The point was not *not* to love but to love *many* people, deeply, as you never could in a single relationship. But now, when Father Tim's head rings with the rector's phrase, the word *discipline* sounds like punishment.

Clutching the railing, he stares into the distance past Grand Cayman, where sea and sky disorientingly merge. He grieves as for a loved one lost at sea, no corpse to bury.

~

He spies the butter sculptor a half second too late to pretend he hasn't.

"Oh, good," calls the artist, who grabs his elbow at the entrance to the Jolly Roger Room. "I hoped you'd come back tonight. Look!" With a flourish, he reveals his new creation. It's Father Tim—the dimpled brow, the thoughtfully canted neck—caught in a look of grudging submission.

The artist, smiling, asks, "Are you happy?"

For a moment, Father Tim is too stunned to understand that the question is aesthetic, not existential. The rendition is so accurately cheerless. "Gee, you're quite talented," he says. He pushes into the bar, to the table where he and Alison chatted two nights ago. The Kalypso Kings break into "Day-O" right on cue. Kip, as though animatronic, performs exactly the same gestures as last time.

The waitress asks if she can bring Father Tim a drink, but he says no, he'll hold out for his friend. He shifts some napkins in a pointless solitaire.

Waiting for Alison: he never handled it well. After their first fuck, she went into the bathroom—she wanted just a sec to clean up—but the closed door was more separation than Tim could bear. He burst in, and they fucked again in the shower.

How easy this is, he thought at the time, how effortless and alive. But could that very ease have been the problem? Growing up with his jilted mother, Tim had come to think of love as a mirage, and so, with Alison, he kept himself from trusting its solidity. But it *was* solid. He sees that now. He wants her again, the wholeness and the heat of being with her. He wants to confide in her, to confess his qualms about being the one to whom others now confess, his panic at the thought of life alone. He burns to lie with her—not just for the physical release but for the stitched-togetherness.

When the waitress returns at quarter past to ask if he's okay, Father Tim requests a Diet Coke. Alison's staff meeting must have run late, he thinks. A foul-up with the Cozumel logistics? (He'd text her, but he never paid the ship's exorbitant data plan. Plus, he hasn't thought to get her number.)

At ten thirty, he orders a double scotch. He asks the waitress to ask the barman if anyone's left a message.

The crowd has thinned, leaving only a half-dozen elderly couples holding arthritic, familiar hands, and at the front a younger pair who rock to the Kalypso Kings' beat. "I feel so break up," Kip inertly sings, "I wanna go home."

At five past eleven, another two scotches downed but not so much drunk as saturated, Father Tim signs his tab. He shuffles toward the exit, by the now abandoned display table, where his likeness is a waxy, melted mess.

~

Thursday's weather is touch and go, no rain yet but a sky the milky blear of a bum eye. Father Tim hunkers in the chaplain's office.

He hasn't eaten. His hangover hammers him with its sharp claw end. At lunchtime, he went looking for Alison, but according to Sandy, the cruise director, she had already gone into Cozumel for the day.

To kill time, and because his mind is too mushy for much else, Father Tim has brought along postcards. The first he addresses collectively to St. Thomas, to the teachers and jealous pals he left behind. Next, his mother. Before embarking, he thought that if the trip was fun, he might sign her up for their New Year's singles' cruise. Now he tells her how much she would hate it: the wastefulness, the enforced merriment.

A faint rapping: a visitor's knock, or maybe the sulky table-slaps of someone losing at poker in Pirate's Cove.

"Hello?" he says, and in comes Les, his face and neck sunburned to the shade of cooked shrimp but his buzzed scalp a halo of lighter flesh. He holds a Pioneer seed cap, worrying its brim into a frown.

"Hi, Father," he says. "Disturbing you?"

"Not at all. That's why I'm here." He motions for Les to sit.

"Case you're wondering," Les says, "she went ashore."

"You didn't want to see Cozumel, too?"

"We had a fight," he says, crimping his cap more firmly. He recounts how, after breakfast, Babs sicked up her food for the third time on the cruise. He helped her back to their cabin and fizzed some Alka-Seltzer, but the trouble wasn't her stomach, she confessed; it was her conscience. She'd been seeing someone else. A woman. Denise.

Les rubs at his reddened neck. "Another *woman*? I'll be doggone. And telling me now, a day before our anniversary?"

"I'm so sorry," says Father Tim. "You must feel blindsided." Not acknowledging he already knew the truth feels like a lie.

"Actually, almost relieved," says Les. "Now at least I have an explanation." But his face, like a cliff suddenly eroding, falls loose. "Oh, Father," he whispers. "Oh, Father."

To be called upon like this by a man his own father's age should validate all he's worked so hard for. But a sense of inadequacy knocks the wind out of him.

"She said I could ask for an annulment," Les goes on. "Said that there's a difference between what *feels* true and what *is*."

Father Tim is humbled to hear his own advice quoted. "And what did you say back to that?" he asks.

"That I would do no such thing," says Les, sitting straighter. "That she's my wife and she always will be."

Father Tim stares at this damaged, stalwart man, revising his evaluation. What struck him initially as stony doltishness he sees now as Les's bedrock strength. Here's a guy who's witnessed the wreckage of countless storms, the terrible routineness of disaster, and still he believes—he's staked his whole life on believing—that you can always rise up and rebuild.

"I know I'm not much to write home about," says Les. "I've never had the looks of some guys." He gestures to Father Tim's musculature. "Maybe I can't be everything to Babs, but I can be a lot. We've put too much into this to scrap it."

This is when Father Tim should bolster Les. Annulment, he should say, is a drastic, last-ditch measure. Better to try all other options first. (Just as a priest who finds himself doubting his vocation should work like crazy not to quit his vows.)

He pictures Babs when she first approached him: boggled, woebegone. And then how she brightened when she spoke about Denise, the film of sorrow skimmed from her expression.

"Please," says Les. "Will you talk to her?"

~

Back in his cabin, he pumps pushups until his arms give out. He flattens onto the floor, his heart going skittery, a compass needle in a magnetic disturbance.

He waits for a call from Alison. And waits.

Finally, after skipping dinner, he goes in search of Babs. He checks the spa, the casino, the Jolly Roger Room, eyes peeled for Alison as well. On the Indulgence Deck, there's a drum show and a contract bridge tournament, but neither woman is anywhere to be found.

Ready to quit, he climbs higher, up to the Liberty Deck, and wends his way aft, toward the railing. In daytime it's where skeet shooters kill their birds of clay, but now it hosts hopeful sunset-lovers. The washed-out sun is veiled by clouds; the crowd is sparse, mumbly with disappointment.

Which is why he's not surprised to find Babs here.

"I did it," she says softly. "I told him."

"I know, I had a talk with Les," he says. "How do you feel?"

"I feel," she says. She presses her chest against the steel railing. "Honestly? Not much. Like how food tastes when you've got a bad cold."

"That's natural," he says. "You're in shock."

"I thought he'd leave me," she says. "But he's made it tougher. He's put the choice on me."

Father Tim winces against the stiff sea wind. "Choosing makes us human," he says. "Knowing that we *have* to choose, because we only get the one life." It's what he tried to tell Alison—and himself—the other day, but now he feels the hairline ache of it in his bones. "If you leave Les," he says, "you'll mourn your old life. If you stay, you'll mourn the life you might've had."

"That's just it," Babs says. "How're you supposed to weigh two things when one's already on the scale and the other . . . well, it's only in your head? I was just thinking, standing here: I don't know Denise's middle name. I don't even know if she's got one." She lets out something between a laugh and a grunt. "Then I think: If I always only stuck with what I know, I never would've married Les to start with. Wouldn't've had my two wonderful kids. Sometimes to get somewhere new, the only way's to jump."

Part of him wants to tell her, *Yes, keep going. Go! Don't turn back from the edge of happiness.* But of course he can't counsel her to violate a sacrament. And who's to say, if she took the leap, happiness is what she'd find? "Sometimes it takes guts," he says, "to stay and stick things out right where you are."

Babs coils a hank of hair around her fingertip; she twists and twists, but it won't hold a shape.

"If you left Les," he asks, "what would you miss most?"

"I'm sick to death of thinking about who I should be for Les. Or for my kids. Even for Denise. I want to be somebody all by myself."

"But Babs," he says. "Nobody is anybody by themselves. Life is with other people, and with God." He turns and stares at the indistinct horizon. The sky's the color of bruised apple flesh.

A tap on his shoulder. A woman holds out her iPhone. "Would you mind?"

Father Tim and Babs both laugh. "An easy mark?" he says.

"Hey, if it's a problem," says the woman.

"No, I'd be happy." He takes her phone. "It's just, I've been asked a lot lately."

She's his age, give or take, in a hot pink halter top; she holds herself with calisthenic poise, like Alison. Beside her stands another woman, also halter-topped. The older sister, Father Tim decides.

"Not much of a sunset," he says. "Still, want me to get it in the background?"

"Perfect," the sisters call in unison.

Father Tim begins his count to three. By "two" the women are locked in an all-or-nothing kiss. Swallowing "three," he taps the screen. *Click.*

The women go on kissing, then finally disengage. "Thanks," says the one in pink. "Our one-year anniversary." They flash fingers with matching rose gold bands.

Smiling at the lovers, Father Tim says, "Congrats," while Babs stands there, silent, gaping with awe or horror. To see what's possible is sometimes worse, he thinks, than being blinkered.

~

At midnight, sleepless, he goes back to the deck, to the same spot where he and Babs stood. He needs the touch of unconditioned air.

The *Destiny* is at sail once more, chugging on its long haul home. It will cruise around Cuba's untouchable western shore and head at last for Fort Lauderdale. He wondered, when the trip began, why a cruise would even need a chaplain. Wasn't the journey's coddled escape consolation enough? But now he sees how freeing yourself from the trap of your routine can set the springs of other, sharper traps.

A crisp moon undermines the privacy of night. The air is fickle with swells of warm and cool. Father Tim faces the sky. He prays.

He prays for Babs, that she'll make the best decision. And for Les, that he won't be left behind. That these two prayers might be mutually exclusive is a puzzle he leaves for God to solve. Let there be more love and less loneliness, he beseeches.

But he's unsure what an answered prayer would be. Does his priest's faith—still sturdy within him, as strong as ever—mean he's got to live a priest's life? Is there room for love of God and someone else?

Then comes the honeyed voice. "Hey, Twinkle."

He sees her first not as a woman but as a flower, an outsized orchid sprouted from the deck. Her evening gown, sheer and shapely, is leaf green at the legs, and at the bust blooms with violet.

"Alison. I didn't hear you coming."

They stand there a long fifteen seconds, just breathing, watching the ship's wake diverge. His pulse beats boldly in his ears. Around Alison's neck hangs a strand of fat pearls; her dress is cut so the gems flirt with her cleavage.

"What's the occasion?" he asks.

"Formal dinner. Captain's table."

The briny air gusts around them, stirring up salt and grit. There's the thin sound of laughter from somewhere up-deck and, far below, the engines' grumbling.

"Last night," she says. She strokes a pearl in the scoop of her neck. "That was gutless. I'm really sorry. It's just you show up, after all these years, a *priest*, but there's still that . . . I don't know, between us. I didn't know how to tell you . . ."

"It's all right," he says. "I'm just glad you found me now."

He says this mostly to soothe her, but as the words come out, he understands they're true. His budding anger, last night's humiliation—it all rolls away like the *Destiny*'s wake.

Standing here now, feeling graced, at the hem of her moonshadow, he's not unconvinced of divinity at work. How much clearer a sign could he expect? He steps into the lee of her tall, exquisite form, her body heat a faint radiance.

"Ah, *there* you are," booms a man's baritone.

They turn back to its source. Andrew, the redheaded trip leader, strides toward them, his dinner jacket catching wind like a sail. "I know, I know," he says, "tour guides should be on time." He grins for a calculated instant, then ducks to land a kiss below her ear.

"Andrew," she says, pulling away, "you know Father Tim?"

"Sure, of course. He was in my group at Ocho Rios." Andrew clamps him in a double-handed shake. "Did you have fun that afternoon?"

Father Tim reclaims his hand. "Came back early," he says.

Andrew drapes his arm around Alison. "Gorgeous!" he says, and it's not clear if he means her or the moon. "What's the plan? More dancing? Champagne?" He whirls on the toes of his wingtips.

Alison tries to smile, but it comes off as a cringe. She looks fretfully at Father Tim.

"Oh, no problem," Andrew says. "Father, you want to tag along?"

"No," says Alison. "This was just an accident. I mean, coincidence. Tim was taking a midnight stroll."

Father Tim says, "Well, I was kind of looking for you." His biceps, still smarting from this afternoon's workout, contract beneath his cooling skin.

A web of silence falls upon them.

Alison says, "The thing I wanted to say . . . we're engaged."

"Proposed at the falls in Ocho Rios!" says Andrew. "Two cruises ago."

Father Tim glances down to her hand, sees the diamond. She must have taken it off for their nightcap. "You couldn't have told me?" he says.

"Was going to. I should have. Just didn't want it to be the *first* thing—like *you* didn't want to be seen right off as celibate. And after that . . . well, it got harder."

It's a chickenshit excuse. As lame as his own defensiveness about celibacy.

Andrew invites him again to come along for ballroom dancing. Father Tim declines. He can't look at Alison. Instead he turns, as the sound of their double footfalls fades, to the railing and its view of the wake. The furls of water widen and widen, two lines that will never intersect.

~

The Wedding Chapel is on the Fantasy Deck, kitty-corner from the duty-free shop. It's a smallish room, painted in sunny stained-glass shades as if to compensate for the absence of windows. Unaccountably, there's an overboiled, industrial-food smell.

The ship's photographer, a schnauzer-faced, fidgety man, caps and uncaps his camera's lens. By the altar, at parade rest, stands Captain Dickerman in a blue uniform with golden epaulets. Father Tim has warned them this will likely be a bust; only one couple paid for the Renewal of Vows package, and that couple is Babs and Les.

They've agreed to wait until ten past. It's already 4:08. The souvenir champagne flutes with the Sun Line Cruises logo sit empty on a silver tray. The commemorative certificate, awaiting the captain's signature, stays stowed in its coral cardboard tube.

"Call it quits?" the photographer suggests. "I have to shoot some 'after' pics at the spa."

Captain Dickerman checks his watch and gives a pouty nod. The photographer collapses his tripod.

"Sorry about the bother," says Father Tim. He thumps his rites book against his palm.

"Father, I've got a theological question," says the captain. "I hear you got the best grades in your class?"

"True," he says, wishing he were slightly worse at tests. Then he could have avoided this whole trip.

"Here's what I've wondered," the captain says. "Wedding vows are for life, right? 'Till death do us part.' So how does a renewal of those vows make any sense? Isn't that conceding that they *aren't* permanent?" The captain bares a cunning, trump-card grin.

Dredging his mind for an answer, Father Tim discovers only jetsam. Right and wrong seem like distant shores. He's about to admit he's stumped when in walk Babs and Les.

"We're in business!" the captain says, and hails back the photographer.

Babs wears a satin dress that's maybe one size too small. Her face is tanned, her hair frosted and teased aloft with spray.

Father Tim touches her shoulder and gets a static shock. "We'd almost given up on you," he says.

She rubs the spot where he touched her. "Me, too."

Les, in his tuxedo, shifts and twists his neck, self-conscious as a Great Dane in a sweater. "Sorry," he says. "Sometimer's again. Couldn't remember where I'd stashed the ring." He hands the captain a small jewelry box.

"Marvelous," says the captain. "What's a cruise without a little 'I do'?"

Wife and husband stand at a measured distance. In her girdling dress, Babs appears breathless. Father Tim sees where tears have streaked her rouge. But when Les takes her hand, she offers a small smile and at long last quietly exhales.

What happened? Father Tim wants to ask. A more responsible priest might halt the proceedings, insist that the couple talk straight. But even if he heard them out, he'd never glimpse the circuitry that keeps alight the filament of marriage. Who is he to question their commitment?

"Can we?" says the photographer. "I've got my other shoot."

The spouses inch closer together with the hopeful awkwardness of blind dates.

Father Tim opens his book. "Repeat after me," he says. "'I renew my commitment to you, my wife.'"

Les matches his cadence word for word.

With text in hand, Father Tim can let his mind drift. He conjures the future, seeing it all too well: the dozens and dozens of weddings he'll be called to oversee, and the others he'll never witness or attend—Alison's wedding to Andrew, his own. He'll be joined to God, and that will have to do.

"'I promise again to be true to you in good times and in bad, in sickness and in health, to love and honor you all the days of my life.'"

Coming from his lips, the pledge isn't binding; when Les repeats it, the words gather weight.

"All right, then," says Father Tim. He turns to Babs. "Ready?"

Uncle Kent

Into the hushed kitchen Kent comes barreling so fast—a train out of a tunnel, pushing forward all that pent-up air—honestly, I think my ears might pop. I don't suppose he could've heard Sammy when she turned to me a sec ago and mildly asked, "Mom, could you?" Her apron's come undone, and her fingers, webbed with egg whites, are too slimy to retie it. It's not really me she needs, only my cleaner hands, but I was scared she'd stopped admitting she needs anything from me. Kent's been here less than a day; could he already have tempered her so much?

But as soon as he's burst in, she steps away from me, her apron strings forgotten. "Wait," she says. "Uncle Kent, what *is* that?"

Peeking out of his tote bag is a battering ram of Brussels sprouts—a full stalk, the newly old-fashioned way they sometimes come now. Sammy peers in, squinting, as if she hasn't seen those things a hundred times before.

"Oh, come on, Sammy," I say. "They sell them like that at Stop & Shop."

She frowns at me extravagantly, the whole spindly length of her glimmering with impudence—it's been getting worse since our fight two nights ago. There's something newly stagey in the way she holds her bony limbs, the way she flicks her swooping, corn-silk bangs. Even her eager little boobs (have they grown in just two days?) appear to be shamelessly performing.

"Maybe she's never noticed?" says Kent, cutting her slack, as always. "Which means, hey! I get to show Samantha something new." (Back in June, at her pool party, the day she turned thirteen, Sammy decreed she'd henceforth be Samantha. Kent's been a pro at humoring her, depending on her mood, letting her play at worldliness or, now, naivete, but I—hopeless, head in the sand—have hung on to my notion of the simple, candid Sammy.) "They're just normal sprouts," he adds. "The way they come from the farm." He snaps off a bud with a satisfying crack, then flourishes it before her. "Voilà!"

"Cool," she says, and bestows on him a supple little laugh, then cleans her eggy hands on her untied apron. "I'd never thought to think of how they grow."

"You're welcome," he says. "What would you do without me?"

~

I'm always a bit jealous of how sweatlessly he charms her, but how could I ever argue with their bond? Even with all he's missed during his stints overseas, he's the one adult who can always get to her: flips her blue funks inside out, turns her gloom to giggles.

He's charmed her like this, and vice versa, since the day she was born. Slumped in my maternity bed, wrung out by her wailing, I thrust the squall of her into his arms. "Here, *you* try," I said, and then, to the baby, "Meet your uncle Kent." He was the saint who'd sat with me throughout the yowling labor, letting me crush his hand with each contraction. He barely had to rock her before Sammy softly cooed. He nosed her raw, red scalp and never flinched.

Without Kent at the hospital, I would've been alone. My mother, since I'd told her I was pregnant, had scarcely deigned to phone, dead set against my having a baby on my own—and with a nameless sperm donor, no less. "A father out of a catalog?" she'd sneered when I first broached the plan. "What, like buying garden seeds from Burpee?" Why the rush, she wanted to know; I wasn't even thirty. "And how're you going to raise it, then? Who'll be there to help? Tell me, not that wretched ex of yours."

But Kent was not just any ex. Ex implies *without*, and Kent was far more *with me* by then, six years after our breakup, than he had ever managed when we were dating. We'd met when I was twenty: too young to buy a beer, let alone to know myself well enough to hold my own against him. His love was like the wooden mold a glassblower fills with melted sand. Could he be blamed for how pliant I was, how pushable into shape? But later, after we both grew out of our weakest inclinations—when I'd become less prone to his (or anybody's) molding, and Kent was sensibly married to someone else—he was finally freed to be the "just a really dear friend" I needed.

Needed because, if you stripped away my mother's shitty tone, what she'd asked was not inconsequential. Who *would* help? Specifically, who'd be a man for Sammy? Not my dad, who'd died when I was eight, a raddled memory. And no blood uncles, since I was an only child. I settled on Kent—forgiving him, forgiving the fledgling I'd been with him—as the man I hoped my daughter would come to count on.

As honorary uncle, he proved better than I'd dared hope. When she was an infant, he loved her, loved her very infant*ness* (actually, more than I did). Diapers didn't faze him: he weighed the full ones in his palm, applauding her hearty output. When she was three and spent all winter cut down by the croup—untold trips to the ER, her rib cracked from coughing—Kent would come and spend the night to let me catch some rest. (Bless his wife, Helen, for never seeming to mind. A better woman than I—or, at least, a more secure one.) Sammy, wired with terror of suffocation, wouldn't sleep. I cried when I held her, her body stiff with fear, and cried at the thought of setting her down. She needed me, of course, as toddlers need their mothers, but I was shocked—sucker-punched—by how I needed her. Kent would have to wrest her from my clasp ("Go nap. Please"), and then he'd run a steaming shower to loosen up her lungs. After I woke, I'd find them, plopped down on the bathroom floor, playing patty-cake with pruney hands.

Helen was older than Kent, but only by three years—certainly could've had kids if she wanted. Her childlessness was a moral stance, in keeping with her life's mission. Peace Corps posting in Cameroon, then Oxfam program officer. "Too many mouths to feed," she'd say. "World hardly needs another." Kent was mostly fine with the choice—that's what he'd signed up for—but he was a fool for kids, a happy, babbling natural. He grabbed at any chance to play with Sammy.

Even for the two years he and Helen lived in Senegal, he aced the job of uncle from afar. (Helen was launching something to do with grain banks for sorghum, and Kent, with his thesis already ages overdue, quit his doctoral program and went along.) At least once a week, he phoned to sing Sammy to sleep. He mailed her birthday cards, and half-birthday cards. Once, he sent a telegram (who knew they still existed?): *Happy 37 Days Till Xmas!*

The spring Sammy was eight, Kent and Helen were back in Boston while Helen earned a Fletcher School degree. We went to their place for Easter, my leery mother in tow. Leery of Kent, still, even after all these years. (She didn't know the details of our split but guessed the worst, having seen how pulled apart I'd been.) I figured she was hoping to find some evidence of unfitness: How could that cad be happily married, and also so good to Sammy, and how could we all get along so well? But everything went splendidly: the spiral ham I brought was sweet; Kent cooked a Senegalese dish called *ceebu jën*, which he translated, to Sammy's utter glee, as "the rice of fish"; and Helen, who could be starchy at times, made everyone feel at home. (I had never not liked Helen—her idealism impressed me—but this was the first occasion I ever truly relaxed with her.)

Kent was in fine fettle, telling Sammy safari tales, teaching her what he claimed to be the mating calls of warthogs. After the meal, he presented her with a foil-wrapped chocolate bunny, somehow rigged so Sammy, when she cracked the hollow treat, found a gleaming silver rabbit pendant. "Look!" she said to my mother. "Grammy, look! It's magic."

"Uncle Kent," my mother said—I almost fell to the floor—"where'd you learn to steal a girl's heart?"

When I tucked Sammy in that night, she twined the pendant's silver chain around and around her thumb. I was about to tell her to be careful, not so tight, when she asked, "How come, if he's not really my uncle, you didn't marry him?"

I didn't know how much she knew—had Mother told her something?—except that he and I had once dated. I decided to act like I'd misunderstood the question. "*Marry* him? You silly goose! He *has* a wife: Aunt Helen." I kissed her good night and hustled out before she might see through my smoke screen.

It made me sad not to be able to tell her our story's good parts, but how could I, without uncanning the worms I wanted to squash as long as possible? (It wasn't only his reputation I wanted to save, but also mine—I wanted her to see me as the superheroic single mom, the savvy owner of Good Hands Massage.) And so I chose to keep to myself the mad dash of memories that Kent's charming magic act fomented: flashbacks to my senior fall, when he TA'd my otherwise mediocre sociology course, Women and Social Change in the Developing World.

This was back when Kent still planned on being a tenured prof, and I was fast-tracked to be a therapist, the kind who uses words, not hands. I found him first: opening day, front of the sloping room. Compelling in the same austere way as Shaker furniture (squarish build; straight, sea-black hair), except for his body's one indulgence: emerald eyes. He saw me staring, and stared back—a beat too long—then winked.

All semester, every class, no matter where I sat, Kent would start by searching me out and . . . *wink!* Tag. You're it.

A week after the last lecture, he summoned me to his office. "So," he said, "now that I'm officially not your teacher . . ."

I was the one who pulled us close. We kissed so hard I went to bed that night with a fat lip.

~

In the kitchen, Kent works his way down the Brussels stalk, sprout by sprout, wreaking decapitations, and Sammy, with every quick green snap, smiles wider. To look at them, you would assume they've never been apart.

In truth, Kent flew in only yesterday from Vietnam.

He and Helen relocated there almost two years ago, when Helen landed her dream job with the UN Development Programme. Kent, who'd discovered his new calling in writing cookbooks, exulted at the chance to live in Asia. "Gour*mutt* cuisine" was his turf, food that honored cultural crossbreeding. (For example, the un-Yule-ish dish he's planned for our big Christmas feast: Brussels sprouts *à la Saigon*, with fish sauce, lime, mint, cilantro, blistering bird's-eye chilis.)

They both said they loved Hanoi: its hectic, rundown beauty, the music of its vendors' constant squabbles. But one morning this August, a motor scooter swerved to miss a stopped ice-delivery cart and skidded up onto the busy sidewalk. Helen, on her way to work, was smashed against the pavement. Died before the ambulance could get there.

Since then, I've lobbied Kent nonstop to move back home. Told him he could stay with us as long as he wants or needs.

No, he's said, he can't—a million excuses why. Something about his lease, and research for his new book. Really, I think, he can't bear to leave the place where Helen last was. Can't bear to contemplate a new life here, without her.

"Come for Christmas, at least," I pressed when we FaceTimed three weeks ago. "Please? You can't spend Christmas alone. *We* don't want to. We need you."

"Dare I ask?" he said. "How goes with Sammy?"

She and I have been wobbly since she entered her terrible teens. She used to be so open, but now she shrouds her feelings; they struggle to the surface in inverse proportion to the zits that flare up daily on her chin.

"I don't know," I told him. "She's getting away from me."

Kent stared, his face eventually falling into shadow as his laptop screen automatically dimmed. He clicked a key, and his face was lit. "Maybe you're right," he said. "I should come."

And here he is, enthralling Sammy, brandishing the Brussels stalk like something ceremonial. (How much does it cost him, I wonder, not to seem like someone still in mourning?) "The shape is sort of—and, well, the color, too," he says. "A Christmas tree? Which, of course, given the occasion . . ."

Sammy beams. "Perfect. Isn't it, Mom?"

Nodding, I continue peeling chestnuts for the stuffing, but a mushy part of me wants to say, *No, not a Christmas tree. Don't you remember your old Little People?* The spherical sprouts, gathered in rows as if for a family portrait, remind me of those two-inch dolls—their jaunty ball-shaped heads—scores of them abandoned now in Sammy's bottom drawer. But how she loved them! Named each one, swaddled them in Kleenex, drew a sprawling family tree to show their lineage. If I blink, that younger, kinship-craving Sammy reappears.

"But Uncle Kent," she presses him now, bouncing on her feet. "Why are there *Brussels* sprouts in *Vietnam*?"

"Think," says Kent. He rat-a-tats a finger on Sammy's temple. His own temples, I've noticed, have grayed a bunch since Helen's death, but he still hardly looks forty-six. "What was the last colonial power in Vietnam?" he asks.

"France?" she tries.

"Exactly! There you go."

"But are Brussels sprouts from . . . I mean, they *aren't*, are they?"

"Aren't what, honey?" he says. "Aren't French? What else would they be?"

"Well, let's see . . . how do you say 'from Brussels'?" Sammy asks, her face aglow with teacher's-pet raptness. As hard as Kent is working not to look like he's in mourning, she can feel his grief, I think, and wants to suck it out of him. Now she taps *his* temple, pretending to be a wiseass. "I mean, shouldn't the sprouts be called"—she flaunts a goading grin—"Brusselsish? Or . . . I know! Brusselsonian!"

Kent yelps a laugh. "Samantha, my love, you're too damn smart. Sometimes I could just eat you up!"

What a relief, I think, as he plonks a kiss between her eyes, to let him work his magic with her, with us. I start chopping the chestnuts, listening to the sound my cleaver makes against the cutting board. *Luck*, it goes. *Luck, luck, luck.*

~

Times like this, it's hard to believe who Kent and I once were. But hearing him in his teacher mode, doggedly quizzing Sammy, also reignites my old sense of irony: of all the places he and I could've gotten together, for God's sake, Women and Social Change?

I wish I could've seen back then the truth I later sensed, that each of us, in studying the subject of forceful women, must've been in search of a corrective. I was seeking an antidote to my brittle mother's power, her years of trying to trim down my dreams. Kent, I think, abashed about his boorish sexual tastes, was hoping, with his academic work, to counteract them.

After our first, fat-lipped kiss, he spent some days romancing me with almost courtly decorum: reciting poems, cooking lavish meals. This was many years before he wrote his first cookbook, let alone thought to beguile my daughter with Brussels sprouts, but he was already artful with his culinary charms. Each meal he concocted was based on a secret theme. My favorite featured lamb tagine and a sweet Spanish liqueur called Grano de Oro. When the theme stumped me, Kent explained that the booze was made from dates. "Get it?" he said. "They're in the tagine, too. I'm dating you!"

But then, soon enough, his molten lust erupted. One time, he barged in to my seminar on ethnicity—a class of only seven of us; where did he get the balls?—to hand me a scribbled note: *Urgent. Must fuck.* Flushing, I excused myself ("Um, family emergency") and we bolted to his office for the best bang of my life.

His tastes, Kent confessed, were "extremely narrow . . . literally. I'm a sucker for ultra-skinny women. And *you*," he added. "Your ribs!" He fitted his fingers into their gaps. "Oh, such perfect bones. You're perfect."

Maybe his brazen confession should have made me cringe, but at the moment I was in shock at the knowledge it provoked: I *liked* being objectified by Kent. I had always been way too thin to qualify as fashionable; the cruelest boys in high school called me "Auschwitz." How many times had my mother clucked her tongue at my pitiful pancake chest, or scoffed at my empty sack of an ass? When she caught me at the vanity once, checking a sweater's fit, she'd said, "Oh, dear, come on, now. You're not that much to look at." But Kent made me feel I *was*: he looked and looked and looked. He loved what I'd believed unlovable.

Gradually he confided more about what turned him on. Not just skinny: skinny and sweet-sixteenish, on the cusp. "Listen, I'm a caveman," he said. "Can't pretend I'm not. But lust is never gonna be PC."

No one had ever shared such unseemly things with me. What did he want, permission? Absolution? "Attraction is one thing," I told him, "but you would never—I mean, sweet *sixteen*?"

"What do you think, I'm nuts? Why would I be telling you this? The guys who *hide* their creepiness—*that's* who you have to watch for."

His honesty seemed so helpless, I found it oddly winning, and safer, as he'd suggested, than other guys' BS. And if, in retrospect, he sounded crude or unoriginal, at the time, the flagrancy of it all felt mostly thrilling: keeping a rich secret from our boringly righteous friends, like vegan activists sneaking off to a pig roast. On top of that, he actually made things *funny*. He treated the dodgy part of himself like a wacky sidekick: Dirty Old Man In Training. (Kent was only twenty-five, and yet he saw the snags he might eventually encounter unless he redirected his desires.) Dirty Old Man In Training—DOMIT, in Kent's shorthand—tagged along everywhere we went. He was a cartoon version of Kent badly misbehaving, a wolf whose eyes popped out on springs when slinky girls passed by. Sometimes, if I asked him where he wanted to go for dinner—the shabu-shabu place in Harvard Square? the Scottish pub?—Kent would pause, then wonder aloud, "Which would DOMIT like? Where do you think the waitresses are more waify?"

Soon, feeling honored by the role of co-conspirator, I would even blithely egg him on. It was as though we shared the same imaginary friend, and we could laugh together at his foibles. One warm day, when the women's track team, in skimpy shorts, dashed past us, I nudged him, saying, "Mmm, I bet DOMIT's doing cartwheels." "Ha!" said Kent. "You know that perv too well."

~

The fight with Sammy, two nights ago:

I'd been out on a date—one of a string in recent months, after years of rarely ever mustering the energy—and I sensed Sammy was sore at having to fight for my attention. If only she knew how bland the dates had been! A dulcimer player with pampered hands, an earnest orthodontist. On this occasion, I'd broken a rule and gone out with a client—he suffered chronic pain from scoliosis—but all during the meal I kept thinking about his back, the blisterlike, old-beef-colored moles along his spine. I couldn't picture touching him there without being paid.

When I got home, I went to her room, feeling guilty for having been gone and missed her tucking-in—or, more truly, nostalgic for the times she would've *wanted* a tucking-in, when she loved nothing more than being half of Mom-and-Sammy. Our cherished bedtime ritual, since she was a toddler: she would lie down, and I would trace her neck, her back, her legs, singing a senseless lullaby of muscles ("Trapezius and supraspinatus, serratus, biceps femoris . . ."). It was our private incantation: by naming her every perfect part, I prayed I might protect her. But lately she'd been skittish, stingy with her body, and I hadn't sung the lullaby in months.

She was in bed but still awake. I sat on the edge of the mattress. Cautiously, I reached to touch her neck ("Semispinalis . . .").

"Don't!" she snapped, whipping away. "Jesus, Mom. Just . . . don't."

I asked her what was wrong. "Angry that I was gone?"

She snickered. Was my guess a mile off?

"Did something happen at school?" I asked. "Something . . . with a boy?" I'd witnessed her, in the past few months, suddenly *seeing* boys, as though the world were a giant one of those figure/ground illusions (*Is it a vase, or is it two facing profiles?*), and all at once her view had shifted, and every boy who crossed her path now blazed with sex potential.

"Was it," I asked, "something with Jacoby?" This was a "friend" she'd mentioned lately, her voice, whenever she uttered his name, full of cotton candy.

She glared at me with new, barbaric eyes.

"Sammy, hon. Sweetie pie. The thing to keep in mind with boys is—"

"Jesus Christ, you think I want advice on boys from *you*? You couldn't even hold on to Uncle Kent."

Was *that* what she thought—and why she'd never asked again what happened with me and him? "Sweetie," I said, "it's not quite that simple."

"And now," she blustered on, "now, when Uncle Kent is finally . . . I mean, he's coming literally *tomorrow*!" She was in such a dither, I doubt she even took in what I'd said. "And you," she yelled, "you go out with some loser?"

~

Oh, Sammy. Does she really hope that Kent and I, with Helen gone, might get back together?

I can't blame her for filling herself up with faulty stories, when I've still not owned up to the true one. But I can't quite blame myself, either. I've so wanted to let her keep her unscathed adoration: this bouncy sprite in the kitchen, kissed on the brow by Kent, his biggest fan.

What would I tell her about the painful way things fell apart? That I, scared of losing Kent, grew ever more obliging—trying to size up what he'd like, then frantically providing it—and he, with my every contrivance, only just got colder? (Had I been but a stand-in for the sweet young things he really craved, and now, was I not innocent enough?) When I bought him front-row seats for the women's gymnastics trials—"Ass-watching seats, for DOMIT's sake," I joked—Kent stiffened and told me he'd be busy that afternoon. It seemed he'd introduced me to his most unguarded self, and then resented how intimately I knew him.

He cut the flow of compliments for my perfect jutting ribs, sniped at me for a prurience he had once encouraged. At the time, I wondered what I'd done to rouse his fury, but looking back, I think his scorn was largely self-directed. He was like the overseer who lashes out at his servant, not because the servant dares to resist but because she doesn't; my acquiescence amplified his guilt.

There came a night—a November night, the ring of impending winter in the air—when we cabbed to Roslindale, to our favorite Dominican hole-in-the-wall, for big bowls of steaming-hot *sancocho*. That morning we had fought, I don't remember why, and I could see that Kent was now trying to make amends. He fished out the ham bone from his soup, the part we both loved best, and placed it, an offering, in my bowl.

I was eager to show him I was ready to move on, too. But how? What should I give to him? My thoughts were still so frazzled from our fight, from all our fighting. Imagining what would mean the most to Kent—or was it DOMIT?—I found myself calling over the wasp-waisted hostess. ("Thin as a wish," Kent had said when we had seen her here before.) My boyfriend, I explained, was enamored by her beauty. "He's noticed you," I said, my voice going skiddy. "And I just wondered . . . I was thinking . . ."

What? What could I possibly have been thinking? That she should join us in bed sometime? Or maybe join just Kent?

I could easily have blurted out something so disgraceful—that's how lost, how in the lurch, I was—but thankfully I never got the chance. The hostess blanched, staring at me as though I'd lost my mind. Hugged her scrawny chest and rushed away.

"What was *that*?" said Kent. "Where's your self-respect?"

I downed some scalding soup, wondering what to say. I couldn't speak. Shame snuffed my breath.

The next week, when I ended things, Kent put up no fight. "I'm sad," he said, "for us, but most of all for you. You should really have dumped me much sooner."

~

But here's the part it might do Sammy good to know when she's ready: that grief, like mine back then, can be a fulcrum; that the hurt I felt, at the end with Kent, eventually led me to good things. To *her*.

Without him, I feared I might wither from my aimlessness, but soon I saw that being with Kent—being the wishful, self-surrendered girl who let him squelch her—was actually what would have done me in. Instead, our breakup pointed me, in perfect serendipity, onto the path that gave me my vocation. During the couple of months when we tried to still be friends, Kent noticed how stressed I was and, spilling over with guilt, bought me a gift certificate for three deep-tissue massages. Lying on the massage table, my aches in someone else's hands, I thought, *This* is what I want to give to other people. Not to analyze their lives, but to touch them—literally touch them. I signed up at the Boston School of Massage.

Massage let me safely fill my need to feel needed—to be giving but not stupidly obeisant. I could dig my thumbs into a client's levator scapulae and revel in her tender sigh of thanks, but after sweaty, brute-strength hours of pummeling other people's pains, I'd end the day lacking for nothing more than my own company.

For the next five years or so, that was how I felt. Then, when I resumed my aching not to be alone, the feeling took a new shape: I wanted to be a mom. I felt it as a pressure at the back of my throat, an urge to moan, whenever I saw a child on someone's shoulders. I carried so many pressing hopes I yearned to pass along, but more and more they felt like liquid seeping through my fingers; I burned to make a vessel to pour them into.

How rash was I for wanting to do the whole thing by myself? I needed advice. Not from my own mother, definitely not. And not from my mawkish girlfriends, who, I guessed, would tell me to wait and pray for Mr. Right.

I longed to talk with someone who'd get my drive for self-reliance but also knew how prone I was to certain weaknesses. I longed, against my better judgment, for Kent.

I thought of asking him out for a fancy-pants dinner—much-belated thanks for the massages he'd sprung for—but chickened out a dozen times without dialing his number. (We hadn't spoken, or even so much as emailed, in forever.) Then one day, at the spa where I worked, a pack of Newports fell from the purse of a Reiki healer colleague. "You *smoke*?" I asked, and she said, "Honey, no, I quit an age ago. I keep 'em to remind me of how much I've changed, you feel me?" I knew then I could handle Kent just fine.

"You sure?" he asked when I called and said I wanted to get together. "I mean, I know how hurt you were and . . . oh, forget it. Yes!"

I picked a jazzy French-Cambodian bistro in Back Bay. When I found Kent out front, I dove in for a hug, but he, I guess, had planned for just a play-it-safe handshake, and ended up jabbing at my kidney.

Over the meal, I caught him up: my spa job, my plans to hang a shingle of my own. "Already picked a name," I said. "Good Hands."

"Wow, congrats," he said. "You're happy?"

"I am," I said, and it felt extra true with him across from me. His sharp face, his emerald eyes: dashing as ever, but now a kicked addiction.

And he, too, unquestionably, seemed happy. Something had settled out of him, like pebbles on a streambed. He said he had just moved in with a wonderful woman, Helen; they planned to get married in September.

I couldn't quell a twinge of vestigial jealousy, but mostly what I felt was relief. "A skinny minnie?" I teased. "How much younger?"

"Almost as thin as you," he said, "but actually, no, she's older. Making an honest man of me at last! And you?" he asked. "Seeing anybody?"

With anyone else, I would've felt embarrassed to confess what I knew must sound more than a little odd. But Kent had been so honest with me about his own oddnesses, I trusted him, somehow, to understand.

I said I wasn't dating, and had no real wish to; what I truly wanted was a kid.

"*Now* I see what this was all about," he said. "You want my sperm?" He laughed the perfect amount, making the notion seem absurd but leaving a bit of room in case, by chance, he'd hit the mark.

Actually, I had considered him—the hair, the eyes, the build—and thought our looks, blended in a child, could be appealing. But no. I wasn't looking for entanglement, least of all with Kent. This was for *me*, the me I'd found only in leaving him.

I laughed more fully than he had. "The only thing I want is your advice." I said I didn't fear the work of raising a kid alone—hard, of course, but I knew I could do it. My real fear was about motivation. Was I just giving in to my old inclinations, succumbing to the need to feel needed?

Children, he assured me, were *meant* to be dependent. That was a healthy thing for me to want. He tested me, though: What if the kid was homely, or sick, or . . . boring?

I said I didn't know—how could you ever know?—but the not-knowing was part of what I liked. That open water.

"Yes, then," he said, smiling. "Yes, I think you're ready." When he raised his wine in toast, his eyes filled with tears. "Sorry, it's just so nice to see you finally . . . being you. I hated how we . . . how *I* . . . God, I was such a prick."

Not a bad person, I thought. Just a bad mate for me.

"No," I said. "I'm sorry, too. I didn't know who I was."

"Please!" he insisted. "Let me win this fight, okay? *I'm* sorry."

Hearing ourselves, our tug-of-war apologies, we cracked up, and suddenly we were friends again, or maybe for the first time—a friendship like the rummy peach flambé we finished dinner with: all the volatile fuel flashed off, leaving just the sweet essential taste.

~

I relish a similar sweetness now, here in the kitchen, prepping our Christmas feast. The soft smell of chestnuts, an earthy whiff of sage, and both my most-adored ones standing close. Sammy, as misguided as she was to want me back with Kent, actually might've gotten something right: with Helen gone (although, for Kent's sake, I wish she weren't), he and Sammy and I make an even tighter unit. A strange one, sure, as muttish as the menus in Kent's cookbooks, but still a kind of miracle of a family. Or maybe I read Sammy wrong—I usually do, these days—and this, just our togetherness, was all she really wanted.

Kent is doubled over, repeating Sammy's corny jokes. "Brusselsish!" he calls. "Ha ha! Brusselsonian!"

I'm sure he wants to hold on to this moment as much as I do, to the softened, unsnarly Sammy, our recent fight forgotten, who pokes his belly impishly, saying, "Right? Am I right?"

"Right," I chime in overbrightly, doing my best to play along. "I mean, no one ever calls them *French* sprouts."

"Well, okay," says Kent. "From this point on, '*Samantha* sprouts.'" His voice brims with easygoing, good-old-sport affection: the model of unconditional uncle-love.

Sammy starts to wag her hips, whipping her untied apron strings coyly back and forth, and when Kent tries to match her, with artless jerks of his hips, she minces about ever more incitingly—*whip, whip*.

That's all it takes—her vampish dance of studied guilelessness—and all at once I see what I've been working so hard to hide from: I see how much of me she has in her.

"Knock it off," I say faintly, as if it's no big deal.

Kent's goofy grin tells me he still hasn't picked up what I've noticed.

But now I can't unsee it, this fawning act of hers, the way she strives to squeeze herself into the shape of what she thinks he wants.

"Sammy," I say, "you've got to get that batter done and bake the cake. I'm going to need the oven space soon."

She scowls at me.

"Samantha!" I yell. "Now!" My voice is so sharp I see Kent's shoulders jump.

"Fine," she says, rolling her eyes. "Whatever you say, *Mom*." Like the name of something fat and dull and old.

Then she looks down, feigning to remember only now: *Oh, what's this? Silly me! My apron*. The strings dangle loose along her twiggy, coltish thighs, the flaps unfurled: a bright bullfighter's cape.

For so long, I've told myself a self-contented story: how brave I was in building just the family I wanted, all the shoals I deftly sailed around. As if my boat didn't from the start have leaky seams. How can I fault Sammy for her sycophantic put-on, after all the long, blinkered years of my pretending? Burying all my qualms about Kent and who I was with him, in order to win the nurturing I needed.

"Uncle Kent," Sammy trills. "Would you do me the honors?" She holds up her clean hands, perfectly capable of tying an apron's strings.

The chestnuts are all chopped. I sweep them into the stuffing, trying to wipe the cutting board with my palm.

Sammy turns and backs up to within an inch of Kent, her eyes giddy with calculation. "Please?" she says poutily. "Could you, Uncle Kent?" She shakes the bell of her butt, a little tinkle.

All of a sudden, his grin's collapsed; his face has gone pasty.

I want to look away. It's all I've ever done.

But Sammy shakes her ass again, and Kent, with a cold-cocked grimace, gapes at it. He reaches for the strings.

Thieves

There were two of them, pssting at me from the murk beneath a palm tree, along the jungly trail that twisted off to the shantytown. In grubby board shorts, shirtless, the slim one sat with a towel around his shoulders. The burly one stood behind, brandishing cordless clippers, and buzzed his friend's blackish hair with tender brutality. Even from thirty feet away, out on the white-sand lane, I could sense the fresh crew cut's effect: his head looked newborn, true. A blank slate.

"Oi," he beckoned. "Oi, brother!" He used the English word but Brazilianized: *broa-der*.

I glimpsed his waving arm, its skinny animation, but not his face, not in any detail. The sky was starting to blur with dusk, and of the scarce streetlamps along this shortcut between the *kombi* stop and our surfside guesthouse, only one gave out any light. I'd watched boys all over the island using such lamps as targets, pelting them with beer bottles and rotting coconuts; when the bulbs burst, the hooligans cheered, "Goal!" But this kid and his roughneck pal were older—eighteen? Nineteen?

"Brother," the slim one called again, his voice sharp with nerve. Then he added, in Portuguese: "Please? We just want to use your cell phone."

This was my third trip to Bahia, after projects in São Tome and Mozambique, and I could handle basic conversations in the language. "Sorry," I said. "Don't have one." I didn't break my stride.

"Liar!" yelled the tough with the clippers, squaring his brawny shoulders. "How stupid do you think we are? Liar!"

A stunted mutt, scared by the shout, bolted from the bushes but just as soon forgot its fear and fervently stole some fish bones from an overflowing wire cage of trash.

"Sure, I have a phone," I said. "Not with me."

"Seriously?" said the lean kid, goadingly rubbing his crew cut. "I thought a gringo always has his iPhone."

Another two hundred yards and I'd be safe at the folksy guesthouse, with its hammock, its icy caipirinhas. I'd suffered a sticky, mosquito-addled day in a boondocks village, dickering with farmers about a loan for their heart-of-palm plantation. No matter that the interest rate was already close to nil, and that my services and the environmental adviser's were pro bono, the farmers wouldn't let up on their haggling. Forget it, then, I wanted to say. Stick with your current pittance. Instead, I grinned my do-gooder grin and told them yes, I understood. Yes, of course, I'd see what I could do.

But now this cheeky, crew-cut punk, his brazen heckle (*gringo!*), had severed the last thread of my politeness. "Carry my phone here?" I said. "Where I might meet a thief?" *Thief* was one of the first words my Portuguese coach had taught me, a satisfying nasal sneer: *ladrão*.

He stood up slowly, smiling, shaking out his towel. Theatrically he snapped it, and the world at once was weaponized: towel, clippers, fists. (Vagner, the guesthouse owner, had warned me about the shantytown; "crack" was all he'd said, all he'd had to.)

"Why are you alone?" said the kid, sauntering halfway toward me. He swept clipped hairs from the hollow of his scrawny, meatless chest. *Just this easily*, he seemed to say, *I could dispense with you.*

I looked ahead, behind: no one on the lane. The only building, a shuttered vacation home from the island's boom days, sat dark behind its wall of concrete studded with jagged glass.

"Why?" he repeated. "Where is your sexy wife?"

"You don't know me," I said, ready to sprint. "Leave me alone."

"No, no, your wife," he said, and staged a vulgar pantomime, swinging his hips, hefting imagined tits. "Where is she today? Where is Marisa?"

I stopped short. Were they stalking her? "How do you know her name?" I said. I took a hard step closer. "Tell me. *How?*"

He didn't flinch; he laughed. "*Now* you defend her? Good!" he said. "Not like yesterday, arguing with her: '*Stop, Marisa. Marisa, please.*'" He sang the words in lilting, malformed English.

The gossipy little tune sapped some of his menace. What had Marisa and I been sparring about, the day before? She'd been overpraising my tact with the local land agent, and I'd been trying to tamp down her sweet talk.

"She's not my wife," I said, guessing he meant no harm. "Just my"—what was the word for coworker? Come on, what was it?—"my friend."

"Oh, a 'friend.' Nice," he said. "Friends can be more . . . fun." He grabbed his crotch and, giving a low grunt, stirred it.

Now *I* was laughing: at the pureness of his swagger, and at his conviction that I—at thirty-eight, balding, plain-faced—was sleeping with a looker like Marisa. Or with any woman, for that matter. I found it—found his cocksure act—impairingly seductive.

"Today she didn't come," I offered. "Sick, you know? Her stomach?"

"*Ai*, the gringos. Always sick! They want so much to taste our island life, but the gut says no. And you?" he said. "Your stomach is hard and strong?"

"Me? Oh, yes." I patted my paunch. "The stomach of a *baiano*."

He nodded warmly, clearly amused I'd called myself a local. He didn't need to know about the prophylactic Cipro I'd been taking twice a day since I arrived (the script written by Craig, my internist husband).

The burly kid approached now, too, revealing his darker face, his broody brow. He paused to squint judgmentally (would he call me a liar again?), then sprang forward, bellowing something. I stiffened, stumbled back. On he barreled with bullish, galumphing charm, his cheeks dimpling. "Come!" he was saying. "Forget the cell phone. Have some coconut. The water is good for you—makes you healthy."

Even now that I got his words, I felt a little shaky. No, I told him, I had to go, they'd miss me at the guesthouse. I should see if Marisa had improved.

"Later," he said dismissively. "You must live!" He opened his arms invitingly, like someone in a travel ad.

The lane was still deserted. Even the dog had fled. My sped-up breaths infused me with a tingle of remoteness. I stood there in the dimming light, letting the island's evening soundtrack throb against my skin: hymning frogs; the sly swish of monkeys in the mango trees; from down the lane, the sea's endless applause.

"Maybe the gringo is just too [something]," the kid with the crew cut said, using a word I didn't recognize.

"Yes, I think," said the bigger one. "Too [something] to be with boys from the street, like us."

"No," I said. "Come on. How can you say that?"

"Well," he said. "Then so?"

The day's heat had dissolved into a briny, pricking breeze. The air itself seemed to egg me on. "I guess . . . ," I said, "I guess, okay," and started down the path.

He punched his muscled arm in the air, huffing a note of triumph. "Jonas," he said, and thumped his chest, by way of introduction.

"Carl," I said, close enough now to shake his rocky hand, and to see the scar, in the shape of a sickle blade, below his ear.

The lean kid gave me a fist bump and a giggly, bright "*Beleza!*"

Beleza was right: the guy was beautiful. Something about him reminded me of the stray who'd nabbed the fish bones. His ribby chest, but more than that—his slinky, antic zeal. Craig, who was black, had schooled me not to liken a person of color's skin to spice, and so I tried not to think of cinnamon or nutmeg. But this kid's shade was less a color, anyway, than a *mood*, like one of those impressionistic names they give to paint: *Tornado*, or *On the Brink*, or *Zoom*.

"Wellington," he said proudly. "My name."

"Wellington? Like the boots?" I said.

He gave me a muddled look, poking his tongue at the hole left by a missing upper tooth.

"The British ones," I added. "The ones—"

"Just call me Well," he said. "Exactly like the word in your language, no?"

He and Jonas exchanged some talk I couldn't understand, a whispered rush of which I only caught "could be" and "later." Then Jonas scampered off to procure a coconut. Wellington stayed with me, insisting I take his seat, one of the flimsy plastic chairs ubiquitous in the bars here, this one yellow, marked with the Skol beer logo. He'd be happy, he indicated, to squat on the sandy ground.

When I sat, the chair buckled. I gasped, flailed for balance.

"Maybe no coconut for you," he said good-naturedly. "Too fat!"

At home, I was a touch plump, but here I felt gargantuan, enthroned above this hunkering origami crane of a kid. "Sorry about the phone," I said. "I really don't have mine on me. If I did, I'd let you make a call."

"No, a phone call? No," he said. "I wanted to use its *light*."

"Its light?"

Yes, he explained: to view the haircut better. "We have a mirror, see?" he said, pulling one from the sand: an icicle-like shard of silvered glass. "Jonas says the cut looks good," he said, "but I never trust him."

As luck would have it, I carried a penlight: along with antibiotics, part of my standard travel kit. "Voilà," I said, unveiling it from my pocket.

"I *knew* you would help," said Wellington. "I knew. I said to Jonas." Directing my aim of the penlight, he held the broken mirror. "And?" he said. "What do you think? Handsome?" He bent his head, rubbing his thumbs along the new-mown hairline, as if testing a whetted blade's bite.

Something else Craig would say to white folks (excepting me): *Keep your snoopy fingers to yourself. Don't touch the hair!* But should I, here, with no one watching? Was that what Wellington wanted? Our gazes met. The penlight made his vital green eyes glow.

Here came Jonas, bounding back, a coconut like a loaded bomb aloft in one raised palm. I turned away from Wellington but caught a final, mirrored glimpse: his tongue's wet tip pulsing where his tooth should have been.

In Jonas's other hand, he flaunted a machete. He sliced the air, gleefully screeching stylized kung fu shrieks, then dropped to his knees next to me, all smiles. He flourished the coconut, this way and that, like a sommelier with a bottle of Châteauneuf-du-Pape.

"Nice and cold?" asked Wellington. "A good one for our guest?"

"Absolutely. The coldest one," said Jonas.

With four chops to the husk, he bared the nut's white tip, then lopped it off and, finessing the machete like an egg spoon, scooped a sipping hole. He granted me the honor of drinking first.

I downed a gulp, cool and sweet and not unpleasantly grassy, then gave the nut back to Jonas.

With boyish solicitude, he asked, "You like?"

I told him it was perfect, the best I'd ever had—and maybe it was, because of where and how I'd come to share it.

"Great!" said Jonas. "You want some more?"

"Please." I held my hand out.

"Okay, then. That will be ten *reais*."

"What?" I said. "You're serious?"

His eyes went grave. "They cost money. You think you can just take?"

Coconuts at the beach went for two or three *reais*.

My lungs felt lanced, useless. Was Wellington in on this, too?

"*Porra!*" he cursed at his pal. "Jonas, are you an idiot? Carl is our *brother*. For him, this should not cost ten *reais*." He flashed his grin. "No, for Carl? *Twenty*."

Wellington, too! A bitter shame came foaming up my throat.

I'd struggled halfway out of the chair, ready to make a break for it, when the boys caught each other's eyes and cackled.

"Oh my God, look at his face," said Wellington. "He believed us!"

"He looks like he would hit us," Jonas said.

"Or *cry*," said Wellington.

Jonas mirthfully feigned some *boo-hoo-hoos*.

Wellington wrested the coconut from Jonas and thrust it toward me. "Take," he said.

I wouldn't. Still too rattled.

"We were only joking," he said. "Treating you like a *baiano*." He forced the coconut into my hands. "This is a gift, you see? A gift! For you, our friend." He used the suffix that made the word mean *big* friend, *true, good* friend—not just an *amigo*, an *amigão*.

"Really?" I said.

"Yes, yes, of course," insisted Jonas.

I smiled provisionally, trying to swallow the rest of my suspicions. "Okay, sorry," I said. "Sorry, I understand." I hated that I'd fallen for their gag, that I'd been ready to.

Wellington said, "Stay calm, okay? We want you here. *Beleza!*" He gripped my knee meaningfully and let his hand remain.

My knee had never housed so many vivid, hopeful nerves. "Thank you for the gift," I said. "I promise: I'll stay calm." But just as I said *calm*, I shook the coconut at him, splashing arcs of water on his cheek.

"*Caralho!*" he screamed, and jocularly tipped me out of the chair.

The coconut squirted loose and the three of us scrambled for it, tumbling together, knocking heads, each, in turn, on top. I thought I heard my shirt rip, or my khakis—who cared?

We wrestled on, our laughter fizzing like sparklers. All of us were panting, wet, rough with stuck-on sand. We smelled like a spill of suntan lotion.

When finally we all gave in, Jonas split the coconut, then cut three chips from the husk to use as spoons. We gorged on the creamy, quivering meat.

"My first food of the day," Jonas said. "I have such hunger!"

"Oh my God, really?" I said. "Here, then. You should finish."

"No," said Wellington. "You are the guest—you eat as much as you like. Besides, I think he maybe lied. I think he ate a big, big piece of bread."

At this, they both doubled over laughing again. Why? How could they find their deprivation funny?

Too self-conscious to eat any more, I handed Jonas my piece.

He pointed to my wedding band. "So," he said, "she knows?"

"Who?" I said.

"Your wife. She knows you come here with another woman?"

Craig had texted, the night before: *Fucked any island studs yet?* Followed by a string of flame and eggplant emojis. I could have tried to explain the truth (my gayness, my open marriage), but why—to expose these boys to a world they'd likely never touch? As if our way of life was some grand and noble gift, without which they'd never know true culture? I shrugged and said, "All of us have to keep *some* secrets, no?"

"Or maybe she worries," Wellington said, "not about Marisa. Maybe she worries you came here for the bread!"

Again their rollicking, incomprehensible laughs. I must have frowned.

"You know what bread is, right?" said Jonas.

"*Pão*? Of course," I said.

"No, not *pão*," said Wellington. "He asked do you know *pau*."

"Spell it?" I said, and he did. I'd never seen the word. But how embarrassing—a beginner's mistake—not to discern the nasalized diphthong.

Jonas scrounged around until he found a fallen mango branch, then snapped off a baseball bat–length stick. "This," he said. "This, here, is a *pau*."

"But also it means," said Wellington. "It means, you know, this." He hitched up the bottom of the left leg of his board shorts, and yanked out his fat, floppy cock.

"Oh!" I said, unable to look away.

I thought he would tuck himself back in; instead he pinched his drooping foreskin and, as though taming a rowdy kitten by the scruff, started whapping his cock against his thigh.

Jonas, tittering, took my penlight and trained it on the action, making cheesy porno-soundtrack noises.

Wellington retracted his foreskin, exposing the wet, pink head, which seemed like a separate, guileless creature. "Now you understand when I say *pau*?"

The way I heard it, I pictured a lights-out cartoon punch: *POW!*

A murmuring, then, in the nearby dark. Intruders? Just the wind?

"Let's go," said Jonas. "Wellington. Enough." He tossed me the penlight, took his machete and clippers, and hurried off.

Wellington stood up, languorously rearranging his shorts.

"Enough!" called Jonas again, behind a veil of leaves.

Wellington winked. "See you tomorrow," he said, and loped away.

~

The next evening, when the *kombi* from the village dropped us off, Marisa started prancing down the sandy shortcut lane, swishing her golden ponytail like a semaphore. I called her back, told her we should probably go the long way, the cobbled road that rambled safely through the tourist district. "Heard there's been some mischief by the shanty-town," I said.

All day, despite trying, I hadn't gotten Wellington out of my mind, and when I did find him, I didn't want her with me. Not only because he would likely look past me and ogle her. What if she tried to bond with me, giggling, poking my ribs: *Oh my gosh, Carl, isn't he just adorbs?* How obvious, then; my cover blown: a pansy with his sidekick. I wanted Wellington to see me as a man with a wife at home. A wife at home and a knockout girlfriend here. (This didn't feel like closetedness but its inverse: liberation.)

We strolled to the town center, past dusty internet cafés and faded stucco storefronts. A saggy-diapered girl kicked a volleyball half her size; beyond, an aged woman in a traditional lace bodice implored us to pay to take our picture with her. You could see how, in better days, the place had been a draw: the old Dutch fort, its turrets shedding whitewash into the sea; the seventeenth-century church with a tree branching out of a belfry window.

As we skirted the central plaza, a wizened man accosted us. "Happy hour," he said in English. "Three caipirinhas, price of one. Come."

"Ooh ooh, let's!" Marisa said with a convert's overenthusiasm, still quite new at being an ex-Mormon.

I didn't want to wait too long to hunt for Wellington, but maybe a little liquid courage wouldn't be so bad. We followed the tout to his beachfront "bar"—a corrugated-tin roof atop four tottery wooden posts—where another old man served us caipirinhas.

I toasted Marisa. "Your first assignment—successful, thanks to you!"

"Aw, I bet you say that to all the gals."

"No, I'm serious." She had softened the stubborn farmers, coaxing them at last to sign the loan. "Where'd you learn that kind of persuasion? They teach that on your mission?"

"Kidding?" she said. "In eighteen months, I didn't make one convert."

She tossed back her drink with a happy little hiccup. I downed mine, too, and called for another round.

"If only those folks could see me," she said.

"Drinking the devil's nectar?"

"Yeah, and with an open homo-*sex*-ual."

A beefy shirtless vendor passed, hawking brazier-charred hunks of cheese. "Mmm," I said, inhaling the smell, and Marisa gave a throaty laugh—wanting, I guessed, to think I'd meant the man.

"My mission companions," she said, "were these prissy, perfect girls, always competing to seem the most pious. And everything, *everything*, you do, you do together, keeping an eagle eye on one another. Except the bathroom—but even then, you're meant to stay in earshot."

"Yikes," I said. "I had no idea."

"Compared with that, this?" she said. "With you? What a relief! To do good stuff but honestly. With someone who's just himself."

The barman brought a basket of tiny, fried, smelt-like fish. "Local specialty. *Pititinga*," he said. "Five *reais*."

"Yum," I said. "We'll take them. And also two more drinks?" Then, when he'd gone: "So cheap! At home, that's what—buck fifty, buck sixty?"

Marisa winced. "Sort of makes you feel like crap, right?"

"Maybe, sure," I said. "But I always remember when Craig and I went down to Buenos Aires: economy tanking, desperate people selling scraps of cardboard. But four pesos to the dollar? *We* were rich. I said to one guy—we'd bought a hand-tied rug from him, for peanuts—I said I felt bad giving him so little for such nice work. Know what he said?"

Marisa turned her face hopefully toward me.

"He said, 'My friend, something is always, always better than nothing.'" I swallowed a crispy *pititinga*—bones, tail, and all.

My third caipirinha came. I watched the big poached sun drip its yolk onto the sea, the fishing boats that bobbed like bathtub toys. I felt deliciously liquefied, ready to surge into the evening's swift, uncharted stream.

Wellington. The River Wellington.

"I've been thinking," Marisa said. "About the next assignment? Maybe the farmers here could make video testimonials, so when we get to Ecuador, the folks there will be able to see—"

"Shh," I said. "Listen. The waves against those boats!"

Dutifully, she listened. Then: "So? What do you think?"

"Yeah," I said. "Write up a proposal when we get back? For now, though . . ." I drained my drink and tapped my watch's face.

"Oh?" she said. "Okay. Guess you're right."

I called for the bill, then left a tip as lavish as my hopes for what came next.

~

At the guesthouse, I kissed Marisa tipsily on both cheeks. "Ferry's at ten tomorrow," I said. "Taxi'll come at nine."

"Right, boss," she said. "Straight to bed for me."

"Me, too. We've earned our beauty rest!"

But as soon as I hit my room, I got busy.

First I took the thumb drives I'd picked up in the village—the environmental adviser's latest run-off guidelines, the site maps our agent had updated—and loaded the files onto my laptop. I emailed them to Briana, my admin assistant in Boston.

Antsy to get back into the night, I quickly cleaned myself—not a full-on shower, just a "ho bath," as Craig called it: washcloth to my pits, neck, and crotch. I changed into my swim trunks, a sleeveless T-shirt, flip-flops. Into the zippered pocket of the trunks I tucked a twenty (best to have *something* to give a robber), then locked my wallet and laptop in the safe.

I slipped out the back door, which opened onto the beach. The sky was clear, with a pale, swollen moon lighting the sandbar, where barefoot boys played two-on-two soccer. A lusty wind whipped up from the water. The alcohol in my veins should have made me crude and stumbly, but my body brimmed with a graceful equilibrium. My blood, my breath, the island air: all one balmy smoothness.

I clambered up the path to the road, pulling on arm-thick vines, and came out on the sandy lane, a quick uphill to the rendezvous. That was the word I sang in my head; it sounded urgent, epic. *A rendezvous with a racy island boy.*

I passed the last inhabited house, its ghostlike laundry dancing. A guard dog growled enviously at the end of a rusty chain. Turning onto the jungly trail, I strained for Wellington's *psst*.

Nothing. I kept padding forward.

Here was the palm tree, and here the wobbly yellow haircut chair, but in it rested Jonas, just Jonas. Head thrown back, hands conducting a tune in his own mind.

"Oi," I called. "Oi, Jonas."

He twitched to attention, jolting up, and dumped something behind him. Then he sprang a step too close and crushed my hand in his. "Oh, how good! Carl!" he said. "My brother." His breath smelled strange, singed, artificially sweet.

"Wellington here?" I asked.

He shrugged. "*I* am here."

"Yes, but—"

"What? I am not enough? You do not like me?" His fleshy, big-browed face looked ready to crumple.

"No, it's not—no," I said. "It's just . . . I came for Wellington."

He sat back in the chair, pouty and inscrutable, but couldn't seem to keep his legs from jittering. He jumped back up, told *me* to sit, then hovered hawkishly near. The too-sweet chemical smell was now stronger, all around me. Looking down, I traced the stink to an empty soda can: hole in its side, scrap of scorched tin foil at the top.

Jonas tore a mango from a nearby tree and bit it, ripping off some rind he spat away. He sucked the fruit—nursed it, really, impatient as an infant. "This is all I have," he said. "Just mangoes. Just *green* mangoes." He thrust the unripe fruit before my eyes.

"You're hungry," I said. "I'm sorry. That's awful."

"Yes," he said. "Maybe you have a few *reais* for me?"

I looked into the gloom of the dense, unyielding woods. "Let's walk into town," I said. "I'll buy some food, okay?" I stood, took a step toward the lane.

"No, no. You want to wait for Wellington, I know. Give me the money. *I* can buy the food."

"I'm not giving you money," I said, eyeing his makeshift crack pipe. "Let's get food. Fish? Maybe pizza?"

"*Porra!*" he swore. He hurled the half-eaten mango at my feet.

I staggered back, straight into Wellington. How had he approached so quietly?

"Careful," he said. "Careful, *amigão*. Are you drunk?"

"No," I said, and all of a sudden, I didn't think I was. His fingers set off flares along my sweaty shoulders' skin. I tasted the limey bite of his cologne.

"Good," he said. "I hope you have a lot of"—he winked—"energy." He wore the same ratty, red board shorts as yesterday. Sweat lightly stippled his bare chest. "Maybe you want to walk to the beach with me?" he said.

"Yes!" I said too quickly, unable to look Jonas in the eye. He had sat back down in the feeble yellow chair, arms crossed, scratching at his elbows.

"I am taking our friend to the beach," Wellington proclaimed, as if repeating news for the hard of hearing.

Grumbling a curse under his breath, Jonas tipped his head back, resuming the pose I'd found him in before.

Wellington led me down the trail, gingerly through the leafy-smelling dimness. We turned onto the sandy lane, toward the ocean's roar. The moonlight magnified him with an incandescent aura. It looked as though a touch from him might shock.

I raced ahead—away from Jonas's seeping fog of guilt—but Wellington lagged. "Calm," he said. "More slowly."

I eased my pace, and Wellington, in turn, slowed even more. He told me he was sorry for being gone when I'd arrived. "I wanted to smell fresh," he said, "but I had no perfume. I had to go and borrow from a friend."

"Nice," I said. "I smelled it right away."

"No, to really smell, you must be closer," he said. "Here." Grabbing my wrist, he pulled me to a halt, then into a hug. He guided my head to bury my face into his wiry neck. I took the chance to sniff for any singed hint of crack, but thank God, no, the scent was like a just-cleaned hotel room.

A sudden thudding, like hoofbeats. Too fast for me to flee.

A jolt—a jagged blow—into my back.

I tore myself from Wellington, and I was facing Jonas, his eyes sparking madly in the moonshine.

"Give me your money. Now!" he screamed. "Everything. Give it to me."

He raised his hand, and I could see the glint of the machete. He held it cocked, his arm flexed, the blade like a beast he had to bridle.

"Come on," he said. "Be smart. Give it all."

My body throbbed—not just where he'd jabbed, but in every cell.

Stepping back, Wellington stared blankly into the distance. Why the fuck was he standing there not helping?

Jonas jerked his arm. The sleek machete lurched.

Twenty *reais*. Less than what I'd paid at the beachfront bar. If he were a stranger, a garden-variety thief, I would have caved. But now I was shouting: "I *tried* to help. I wanted to. I wanted!" In Portuguese, I couldn't describe my mournful anger's shape. Maybe in English I'd have done no better. "I tried," I said. "And *this* is how you treat me?"

Jonas glared and set his jaw. Wellington still said nothing.

"Like this?" I yelled at Jonas, and lunged in his direction. "Fine," I said. "Then cut me. Cut me, if you want." I thrust my arms out, palms up, exposing my pallid wrists.

He pumped his arm, and I turned my face, bracing for the gash, but Wellington leapt between us. He thwacked Jonas's ear.

"Beat it," he said. "Idiot! Go away!"

Jonas's hand fell to his side. The blade bit into the sand. He seemed about to snarl something, but Wellington shot him a caustic look. He spat and sped away into the night.

I should have been shaken, but all I felt was thrumming thrill, relief. "Thank you," I said to Wellington. I clutched his neck. "Thanks!"

I couldn't think. I was almost concussed with adrenaline. "Come on," I said, tugging him forward, breakneck down the path.

He stopped. "The beach is *that* way."

"No," I said, "my guesthouse," fearing that if we stayed out here, Jonas might come back.

Wellington twisted his toes in the sand. "Maybe tomorrow?" he said.

"No, I leave in the morning. You're worried about the owner?" Guys like him were regularly hassled by local merchants. "It's fine," I said. "Really. You're with me."

"And your 'friend'?"

"Asleep," I said. "In her own room. Let's go."

Everything now seemed to unspool in double time: our dash down the path, my fumble with the sticky guesthouse key. We tiptoed through the shadowy hall, past the muffled Globo newscast coming from the office.

Inside my room, we hopped around, bonded by a giddy, monkeyish sense of disobedience. My lungs thumped. My pulsing hands and feet felt fattened, potent. I was drunk again—not on booze but on near-escape and sharp anticipation.

I pushed him down to the bed, but he bounded right back up. "Like *this*," he said, and pressed my shoulders until I knelt below him.

When I yanked his shorts, the Velcro fly gave way with a crunching rip. His cock was hard and curved, the color of kiln-baked clay. It had the look of an ancient tool unearthed by archaeologists. I wanted him to dig with it inside me.

I pressed my face into the smother of cheap perfume. I was touched to think of him primping, dousing these parts for me, to cover up his smell of poverty: sweat and grime and palm oil, the faintest trace of piss.

"Go on," he said, pinching my jaw open. With a laborer's deft efficiency, he filled me in one stab. I loved the way he handled me, thumbs hard at my ears, as though I were a tricky apparatus that needed steering. Clapping his fingers tighter, he made a high, uncertain sound, and needled the back of my throat with warm spurts.

He had lasted maybe sixty seconds.

I wasn't disappointed; if anything, I was all the more turned on. How honest and uncomplicated his sprint to gratification! How flagrantly he plundered what he wanted!

"And me?" I said, getting up.

"Fine," he said. "No problem." But he just stood there, noodling with his foreskin.

I opened my shorts and started stroking, abashed but also goaded by his aloofness. He watched with what seemed a kind of professional curiosity, a craftsman comparing methods of production. After a few minutes, he said, "Why does it take so *long*?" I made a stricken face, and he added, in a tempered voice, "If you like, okay, you can touch."

His cock drooped from his fly, dramatically flabby, languid, but what I yearned to touch was his hair: the bristles of his one-day-old crew cut. I reached up and rubbed my palm against its rough preciseness, and in another instant, I was done.

We fixed our clothes, I wiped the floor, we took turns in the bathroom. I figured he might hurry off, but he dawdled, fingering the carefully rustic furniture, and finally sat firmly on the bed.

"I think I still want something," he said.

"Wow," I said. "Already?" At his age, I guessed, he was raring to go back at it; at mine, I was done . . . but I could certainly get on my knees again.

"Normally, in the evening," he said, "I sell popsicles. At the plaza."

I waited for him to go on, but he just stared, hands on hips, as though he'd clinched an irrefutable case. "Okay, um . . . popsicles?" I said.

"Yes," he said, "but tonight—tonight I was here, with you. And so I earned nothing. Understand?"

"Oh," I said. "Oh!" I felt as suddenly foolish as the hollow sound I bleated. "But you never," I said. "I mean, I thought . . ." What? What had I thought?

"A whole night," he said, shaking his finger. "Because of you."

Thunderheads of shame and anger gathered in the distance, but I willed up a wind to ward them off. I liked Wellington's pluck. He'd saved me from Jonas; I owed him. Plus, if I gave him something, it wouldn't quite be for sex—more like compensation for his opportunity cost. That was the concept he'd pitched to me, even if he couldn't name it, and I was tickled to think how well he might succeed in b-school. Shouldn't the kid's entrepreneurial gumption count for something?

"Here," I said, unzipping my pocket. I handed him a bill.

"Twenty?" he said. He crumpled it in his fist. "Twenty is little."

"It's all I have."

He snorted.

"Really, you can check," I said. I tapped my hips, permission for a pat-down.

"You must have more somewhere," he said.

"Told you, we leave tomorrow. I already got rid of my *reais*."

Now he stood. His face was measurably hardened.

I doubted he'd be violent; he knew I could summon the owner. But I felt shitty for fibbing. (Of course I had more cash. My wallet, in the safe, was thick with dollars.) Also, I wanted our interaction not to end like this—as confirmation, for each of us, of our worst preconceptions.

"Look," I said, "I wanted to ask. About what happened before. Is Jonas actually hungry? Or does he just want money to buy crack?"

He looked as though he wanted to slap the question from my mouth. "I *work*," he said. "I *earn*. You saw *me* take drugs? No."

"No, of course, I wasn't saying . . . I'm asking about Jonas."

"Is Jonas hungry? Of course." He poked his belly. "We all are."

"In that case, I'm happy to get some food for him," I said. "I meant it, before. Maybe you'd like some, too?"

Appraisingly, he eyed me. "Food?" he asked. "From where?"

"From here. They'll never miss it."

Now he grinned—grateful, of course, but also somehow impish. Maybe he liked the thought of pulling a fast one on the owner, a man from whom he'd probably gotten grief. "If you would like to give," he said, "then yes."

"Quiet," I said, and motioned for him to follow.

We skulked down to the breakfast room—a stale smell of coffee grounds, crumbs—where I rooted in the cabinet for a trash bag. Wellington watched as I filled the bag with fruit from the sideboard's bowl: a big papaya, bananas, two handfuls of pitangas. When I tossed in some individual boxes of Sucrilhos, the Brazilian version of Frosted Flakes, I saw Wellington's grin go wide again.

I was beaming, too, with righteous, Robin Hoodish satisfaction. What a night! We'd come so close to disaster, but here I'd found a way that we all could end up contented. My heart bulged with leniency—for Wellington, for Jonas, for myself.

Last, I grabbed a couple of rolls, baked by the guesthouse cook—from yesterday, but surely fresh enough.

"Perfect," Wellington jested. "You know how much I like to eat *bread*."

"Here in Bahia, the *pau*," I said, purposely mispronouncing, "is rumored to be very, very tasty." I handed him the ample goody bag.

I hoped he might come back to my room—another minute, at least!—now that things were good again between us, but he scuffled out to the hallway, toward the door. He seemed edgy—embarrassed, I supposed, by his own neediness, the proof of which now dangled from his hand. "Thanks," he said. "I will bring this right away to Jonas."

"Great," I said. "Glad it all worked out."

He offered me a fist bump, then seemed to reconsider, and clasped me in a masculine, endearingly chaste hug. "My brother!" he said. "Your wife is a very lucky woman. I hope you get home safe to her, and happy."

When he nudged the door open, I softly said good-bye.

"No," he whispered. "We never say 'Good-bye.' Say 'See you later.'"

"Right," I said. "Better. See you later!"

But he may not have heard me, he ran away so fast.

I shut the door, smelling him still, his evergreen cologne. I moseyed back to my room, drained but also restored, and minutes later was sprawled in bed, ready to dream brilliant, easy dreams.

~

The taxi was outside, idling, when Vagner, the guesthouse owner, appeared in my doorway, breathless.

"Just a sec," I told him. "One more bag to zip."

Vagner nodded but held his ground. He narrowed his dismal eyes. "Local boy's out front," he said. "Claims he found something of yours on the lane."

Found something? What could I have lost?

Maybe Wellington was eager to give me his contact info and needed a pretext to get past the owner. Or Jonas. It could be Jonas—to thank me for the food, to say sorry.

"All right," I said. "Thanks. I'll go see him."

"I'll go with you," said Vagner. "You know they can be dangerous."

They. How dare he? "No," I said. "I'll handle this on my own."

With disapproving huffs, he trailed me down the hall, and finally said, "You'll speak outside. I'll be at the door."

Wellington stood mildly in the stinging morning sun. He wore a Chicago Bulls cap, a tank top reading, in glittered letters, STREET WEAR—his version of dressed up, I imagined. My throat filled with the memory of last night.

"Good day, Senhor," he greeted me with stagey, clipped refinement.

"What a pleasant surprise," I said. "Didn't think I'd get to see you again."

"Yes," he said. "I think we have some business." He shifted his shoulders, a combination of skittishness and defiance. "I found these on the lane," he said, holding out his palm, in which were balanced two black-plastic thumb drives.

But no, I thought, those couldn't be mine, I had mine in my room last night, and—

"Oh?" I said with trumped-up calm, conscious of Vagner behind me.

Wellington flashed his same old impish grin—the little phony! In the breakfast room, and after, as we'd hugged: he'd had the drives.

"I thought maybe you would like to give a reward," he said. "For finding them. Bringing them back to you."

"Really?" I said. "A reward?" I stared at his open palm. Did he think my very dignity was for sale? "But no," I said. "I don't think they're mine."

He looked confused, his eyes a blur. High on crack, no doubt. "Yes, Senhor," he said. "I know these things are yours."

"How?" I said.

"You *know* how." A scornful, slow-mo wink.

To make a joke of my sympathy! To mock my good intentions! "Why would you do it?" I said. "Did I hurt you? Did I steal anything of yours?"

Wellington shuffled back a step, clenching his fist on the thumb drives.

"In my own country, you know, I'm not dumb," I said. "I'm smart. I help people. That's what I do. I help." The words came out weaker than I wanted.

"In your country, of course," he said, "your life is very nice. A very beautiful, normal life—you want to keep it, yes? That is why I think you will buy these things from me."

"Buy what?" I heard, and turned to see Marisa with her suitcase. "My Portuguese," she apologized. "I couldn't catch it all."

Vagner had come out with her, clutching a phone like a shiv. "Pay him," he said. "That's the way things work here, understand?"

"Wait, you *know* this kid?" she said. "You took something of his?"

"Jesus, no. He took something of *mine*. He stole my thumb drives."

"But why was he . . . what were you even—"

"You made a mistake," said Vagner. "Pay the boy. We don't want any trouble."

"Fine," I said to Wellington. "Let me see those drives."

"Money," he said. "You have to give me money."

"Yes, but first I have to see you haven't damaged them. I have to make sure they're in good shape."

Churlishly, as if he were conferring a big favor, he dumped the drives into my hand. I didn't even look. I flung them to the ground. Then I stomped, and stomped again. The pop of cracking plastic. I crushed the shards beneath my twisting heel.

Wellington's bony shoulder flinched, but he snickered, tossed his chin. "Look," he said. "Look, I have *this*, too." From his shorts he pulled a luggage tag, then waved it at my face. "Your address, see? Your number. I could call your wife and tell her all we did together. Your wife—would she like to hear all that?"

Marisa stared, steely. "Your wife? Did he say *wife*? What kind of lies—"

"We're late," I said. "Get in the taxi. Now."

Then, to Vagner: "Call the police. Tell them he's a thief."

When Vagner started to dial the phone, Wellington spun and ran. His feet slapped and slapped against the sand.

~

Marisa, in the hurtling cab, sat cross-armed. "What the hell?"

"Please," I said. "Can we just get out of here?"

"But what about . . . what about the thumb drives?"

"Sent the files to Briana," I said. "Everything's all backed up."

"Ah, of course." She smiled tightly. "I get it. No harm, no foul."

"Forget it," I said. "That's what I plan to do."

With a lash of her sun-bleached ponytail, she turned her back on me. "But the kid," she said in a sharp, low voice. "Surely you gave him *something*? I mean, something's always better than nothing."

I stared out the window at the blear of passing palms. My left heel, the one I'd used to smash the drives, was sore. I couldn't shake the feeling of something stuck beneath it. I checked and checked but couldn't find a thing.

Stud

This was my hometown: Northampton, Mass. NoHo, the yuppifiers called it, hipping it up like some Big Apple of the north, but we changed it to No ho's, as in you couldn't get laid even for money, or No ho ho, as in this town's punch line sucks. I was seventeen. Weekends and plenty of school nights I bussed tables at Woody's Music Hall.

It was my first job, not counting shoveling for old ladies after snow. The '91 recession had technically just ended, but my mom got canned (was there suddenly less data to be entered?), and I was hustling to keep us off food stamps. It wasn't totally bad, though. Could almost even be fun. They had shows that they served dinner during—sometimes jazz, sometimes folk, sometimes blues—so you could groove while you were clearing people's mess.

FYI: different music, different mess. A blues crowd, if the act was, say, Luther "Guitar Junior" Johnson, was beer and nachos, beer and nachos, fast as we could bring 'em. It's tough to snatch bottles without clanging up a storm, but that music?—not like anyone noticed. Jazz would have us hush-hushing on tiptoes all night long, clearing away *salmon en croûte*, etcetera. Wine glasses, then muddy demitasses. My favorite were the folkies. They'd have their dirty plates stacked and ready, forks and knives in piles, 'cause they themselves had once toiled in the quote-unquote food-service industry, so they empathized.

One Thursday it's a singer/songwriter, never heard of her, Cecilia Mays. "Sensuously smart," claims the poster, a quote from some paper in Topeka. Her CD's blah title: *I'll Call You*. I walk in as they're doing the sound check, and there she is, I assume it's her, on stage.

The hair is what I noticed first. Trick of the lighting, maybe? A fizzy, amped-up halo sort of glow. But this was sound check—they hadn't done lights yet. She was tall and stretchy-armed, you could maybe say cowgirlish, like she'd know a thing or two about hogtying. Legs so long I thought of antidisestablishmentarianism.

Her age I had no idea. Parts of her looked totally grown-up, motherly even, but she had pink barrettes in her hair and a Boy Scout thingy tied around her neck. It was like if you took a full deck of people's fantasies and shuffled them and dealt them all at once.

"Again," called the techie at the soundboard.

Ceel—that was what she told me later to call her—leaned up and kissed her lips to the mike. Clenched her eyes like flinching from a shot. "Mary had a little lamb," she sang, "little lamb, little lamb"—the dumbest song of all time, but her voice! Like someone had struck a match. Raspy to start, then clean blue perfect flame. "Mary had a little lamb, its fleece was white as snow."

"Hold it," the sound guy said, tweaking his knobs. He had a mustache and he tweaked its left tip, too. "Okay, again?"

When Ceel looked about to start, she saw me. Me, tying on my busboy's apron. She paused, like just a sixteenth note, then sang: "You've made me so very happy, I'm so glad you came into my life."

Fuckin' A!

This was a levels check, she was just doodling, but it was easily the awesomest human sound I'd ever heard. Except for my own voice, inside my dreams.

"Once more," the pinhead techie said.

Ballsier, even, this time, she belted out the line. "You've made me so very happy, I'm so glad you came into my life."

When she sang, she looked right at me, and I know this'll sound dumb but I had a feeling—I couldn't have told it to you then, but two months ago they did this thing to my mom, angioplasty, where they stuck a tube into one of her arteries and inflated it to make more room for blood. That's what Ceel did to me, just with her eyes. It hurt a sec, then *zam!* My heart was twice as wide.

Folks don't think I'm good-looking, okay? Not unless they like geometry problems. By high school I was used to jokes about combing my hair with an eggbeater and being the guy who made Picasso come up with cubism. We did this poetry unit in English, and one exercise was "Pick a word to describe yourself." It stumped me, then finally I said I didn't know which exactly, but it was one of those twisted, wig-out words you see in Welsh—a mess of consonants jammed with too few vowels.

I wondered if I'd ever touch a girl. There was this one, sophomore year, who I thought liked me in terms of, you know, "like." Her name was Cass and she stared at me in chem. While magnesium strips were flaring and Bunsen burners were Bunsening, she stared with just-a-snitch-too-wide-set eyes. When I looked back, she didn't look away. Cool, I thought, she's dispensed with all the girly-girl charade, maybe here at last I've got a shot. One day we were assigned to be lab partners. We gabbed and gabbed, distilling ethanol, and I said something about her stares. She laughed just like the gurgle in the test tubes.

Turned out she'd been watching me 'cause I was "off-kilter." That's the word she used. I had an "interestingly off-kilter countenance." Said I reminded her of a basenji, which I had to look up and which turns out to be some sort of dog. Thanks a lot, Cass! That's not even a metaphor. *You're a dog.*

What she was referring to I guess was my ears: basenjis, according to the photo I found in Webster's, have huge ones and so do I. I thought for a while it was a growth-spurt thing, that my ears were too big for my skull and my feet were too big for my legs and my nose was too big for everything, but eventually I'd catch up to myself. But now I'm much older, and still I'm disproportionate. Which in only one way, wink-wink, is a bonus.

When the techie said, "Thanks, Ceel, you're all set," I was on my way back to the kitchen. Shaky, sort of, 'cause of that sudden open-sesame rush of blood, wondering if this singer lady had seen the basenji resemblance, or had she possibly noticed something else? Shaky, too, to be honest, from the Vivarins I'd chased with Robitussin, 'cause this kid said it made you roll like X. It's the drugs talking, I told myself. The drugs. No way she's flirting.

Busboys at Woody's set the tables: flatware, salt and pepper, candle lamps. We folded napkins and married ketchup bottles, and then, if we had time, premade salads. I saw Luke, my manager, and asked him what was down. He said ketchup, and I was like, psych!, 'cause you can make believe it's a *Guinness Book* contest, balancing the most Heinzes of all time. The crowd goes wild, etcetera. But shaky like this, would I be able?

I'd grabbed the tray of ketchups when I heard "Hey." I turned and there she was. Her hair still had this eerie northern-lightsish sort of shine. She stood a good three inches up on me.

"Hey," she said again. "What's your name?"

My name, which now I think is pretty cool but back then used to drive me nuts, is Shem. People always get it wrong. They guess "Shame?" or "Jam?" or just knot their eyebrows. But Ceel, she nailed it off the bat.

"Shem," she said. "Like 'name' in Hebrew, right?"

I mumbled something about yeah, sort of, like what you call God since his real name can't be spoken. Goofy, but my mom thought it was cool. And that's when I asked her if she's Jewish.

She giggled, plumped her blond hair. "Me? Nope. Pure shiksa. But somehow I always find my way to Jewish folks. Guess you'd have to call me a Hebrophile." She rubbed her thumb down the ridge of my nose, super slow. "And what," she said, sticking out her tongue, "is *this* about?" She tapped the tip so I'd know she meant my stud.

I'd gotten pierced a couple months before. What it was about was distraction, so people would have something besides my face to focus on. Distraction for me, too: I could twiddle the stud instead of fooling around down south, which at that age, and still now, to be completely honest, I was dying to do all the time.

"It's new," I said, dodging her question. "Newish."

"So you haven't put it to good use yet?"

I shrugged.

"Well," she said, "we'll have to do something about that."

Luke appeared behind her giving me the hairy eyeball, like, *The help shouldn't mingle with the talent*. But at Woody's the performer's always right was their big rule, so I eyed him back, like, *This was* her *idea*.

Still, I said, "Ms. Mays, I'd better get to work."

"Cecilia," she said. "Just call me Ceel. Can I ask you to do something for me, Shem?"

I nodded. What wouldn't I do for her?

"Between sets I'm gonna want two shots of Cuervo Gold. Actually, doubles. Could you bring them down to me?"

There's like a hierarchy, so I said, "I should get a waiter for you. Usually, it's not part of my job."

She stroked my nose again. "Tonight it is."

~

My high was nothing much, more of a middle. By showtime it was like a roulette wheel unblurring and you wonder where the ball's gonna land.

From the food orders, I pegged the crowd as two parts folky, one part jazz, which I therefore guessed would be Ceel's singing style. She came out with a battered twelve-string and fired up this kickass instrumental. Weird, unheard-of half-breed stuff, like an old-time Irish jig going down on Charlie Parker. Everyone in the place forgot to chew.

When she started singing, there was that voice again, not so much a sound as just a feeling: bourbon burning your throat, or sunlight filling your eyes up with tears. She made me think thoughts like that, goofy poem thoughts. Bussing, I couldn't pay enough attention to the lyrics, but there was something about "the bloodshot sunset of your stare" and a chorus that went "You're so mean, you're so mine, hit me perfect every time." She sang like there was a knife held at her neck.

~

Okay, the performers' lounge? Downstairs, near the johns. A grungy old couch and a thin remnant rug and a sink with a mildew-zitted mirror, which if you ask me is like rich folks wearing jeans full of rips. Like, *We're so loaded it doesn't matter how we dress*. At Woody's it was *We're too cool to suck up to the stars*. Not that stars per se were on our concert circuit, but there were photos of Lyle Lovett and Tracy Chapman on the walls, plenty of folks who later hit it big.

I had only been down there after shows, sweeping up. But I told Luke about Ceel's asking me specific, so here I was, two Cuervos on my tray. Fraidy-shaking, Richter six-point-nine.

"Knock-knock." I said it, since my hands were on the tray.

She let me in and shut the door. Took both the glasses from the tray. "Here," she said, handing me one and clicking hers against it, the sound like dice in a craps player's palm.

"Not supposed to drink during my shift," I almost said, or "I shouldn't," or something just as lame, but she called, "Go!" and down the hatch it went.

She looked different now. Her skin? Performing had done something, how a hot shower opens up your pores. Her shirt was undone three buttons, and I wondered if I'd caught her in the middle of getting changed. Sweat streaks at her sides had the shape of lightning bolts.

"Has anyone ever told you," she asked, "how beautiful you are?"

"No," I answered honestly.

"You are. You're so fucking gorgeous."

Quick like a snake she came at me, her lips around my nose. Covered up my mouth too with her hand. I couldn't breathe, and yanked her hand, but she was strong from strumming. She had me muffled, shrink-wrapped with her skin.

"No," I yelped. It came out more like "Wow."

My lungs were crisp with lack of breath. I tugged her hand again. But something in the hotness of her mouth said just relax. Her tongue felt like *Shh, it's okay*. Somehow then she breathed for me, blowing into my nose, letting me exhale into her mouth. Our breath made figure eights, infinities.

When she let go, I thought it would be a relief, but it wasn't. Breathing by myself had lost its point. Then, into my ear, she blew these slow, silky sounds. "Beautiful beautiful beautiful," she whispered as she blew, "beautiful," like that was just her breath.

"The whole time I was singing," she said, "I watched the way you hold yourself. You don't even have a clue about your stunningness."

"This girl said I look like a basenji," I tried to say, but Ceel pushed me down and made me kneel. "Open them," she said, meaning her jeans.

I unzipped her and pulled the fabric down. My fingers shook.

She took my index finger like a pen between her own and moved it in small loops inside herself. The word *autograph* popped into my head. "There," she said and suddenly quit tracing. It was the same size and shape of my piercing's silver ball. "There," she said again. "Now use your tongue."

And so my mouth was on her and I flicked the metal stud. Tickled it against its little twin. I blew out while I did it, breathing "beautiful" just like she had. She pinched and pinched the scruff of my neck. It killed.

When she was done, she lifted me up and licked my lips all clean. "See?" she said. "You see how good you are?"

Then she smiled and knelt and undid me. "Oh," she said, "oh, yes! I had a hunch." She pulled it out. "I'm always right," she said. "The nose knows."

She used her lips and tongue and blazing breath. Her prickly hair spilled all around me. I felt like I was on a bed of coals, voodoo-walking. Like I was holy. Getting away with murder.

"You're perfect raw," she said. "Just the way God made you." She took a bite that left four red marks.

I was close, which I guess she knew 'cause she spun me toward the mirror. "Watch your face," she said. "Are you watching?"

I hate mirrors, but now I forced myself.

I pushed way down her throat, way way past impossible, and I could swear I felt her voice, her fucking *voice*, around me. I was in the place that made her songs.

Thinking of that—that she'd let me into the place that made her *her*—I knew I couldn't hold it in much longer.

She paused for air. "Watch," she said. "Keep watching!"

When she swallowed me again, I went bleary, then refocused, and all of a sudden I faced a new face. As if she'd dunked my skin into a vat of magic liquid, and *zam!* The invisible ink came through. The secret that had been there all along.

"See?" she said after. "Beautiful."

She'd done this kickass thing to me, this revelation thing, but I also felt I'd done it to myself. I was seventeen. I thought I'd just been born.

"Ms. Mays," said Luke, beyond the door. "Five minutes."

We zipped up and splashed our faces clean.

Cuervo on my breath, which I worried Luke might smell, and something sharp I hoped would always stay.

"Ceel," I said.

She raised a stop-sign palm. "Don't forget," she said. "Just don't forget."

She opened the door, but Luke was gone. A different guy stood staring at the floor. He looked up, and this saying of my mom's came to mind: "Throwing good money after bad." He'd bought high, sold low, was how this guy appeared.

"Evan?" said Ceel. "But you said tomorrow."

"Dinner got canceled," he said. "Thought I'd do the drive when there's no traffic."

"Well . . . great, then," she told him. "What a nice surprise." She said it in a businessy politeness sort of voice—I figured he must be her manager. But she walked to him and planted a big kiss smack on his lips, a kiss that must've tasted all of me. "Missed you, babe," she said. "Missed you hard."

His face woke up, a brand-new-penny gleam. I thought of "You're so mean, you're so mine." Was she gonna introduce me? She just kissed him again, then started up the stairs holding his hand. After two steps, she stopped and turned to me. "Hey, Shem, can you have them put some seltzer on the stage? I think I feel a tickle in my throat."

That was the last I'd ever hear from her.

She looked at me, or close to me, sort of hard to tell, a couple of times during the second set. But afterward I had to turn the chairs all up and mop. By then she was gone with what's-his-name.

The next day, I stole into Luke's files and snuck her number. I called, left a message with my info. And called again, every few weeks, despite her never answering, just to hear the voice on her machine.

The last time I tried was two or three years later, when "His Name Was Shame" was climbing up the charts. Some PR-sounding lady picked up, and I was too embarrassed to explain. She offered to send a photo. I said nah.

But none of that, to be honest, really mattered. Not as I watched Ceel from the performers' lounge doorway, tasting my own future on my tongue. She'd said not to forget, and you bet I fucking wouldn't. Every single time I saw a mirror, I would remember. *Tick tick tick*, went the stud against my teeth, a clock keeping some new kind of time.

Do Us Part

The night of the day they were married was the first time she ever didn't want to. She was beat from the smiling and the small talk, waltz after waltz with newly minted in-laws. When the limo finally dropped them at the Copley, the thing she wanted most of all was sleep. Fishy-sounding, she knew, to say "I'm tired" on their wedding night (hardly better than "Sorry, got a headache"). What else could she say, though? How could she explain? For months, she'd invested the event with outsized magic, baffling herself with retrogressive, teenage-girlish hopes (it was the year 2000; could any woman still believe in sparkling ever-afters?). But now, crossing the threshold of the pricey honeymoon suite, what she craved had little to do with bridal-guide clichés of flushed, breathless, special-occasion bliss. No, what she wanted was the start of something longer—of a comfy married complacency, of never again having to feel she had to strive so hard to win him over.

She shucked her dress and draped it on a stiff wingback chair, then shuffled to the multi-mirrored bathroom. She'd peed and was taking out her contacts when six of him came at her from different angles. Then just one: the one who reached around, whose fingers tickled circles through her bra.

"Later," she said, and elbowed him away. "In the morning?"

She hadn't meant to jab so hard. She wrestled again with how she might express an explanation—nothing bad; something good, in fact; a new contentment—but better for now, she thought, just to offer reassurance. "I love you," she said. "I do. You know that, right?"

She wore his ring, and he wore hers. They were wife and husband.

~

That night he fucked her, also a first, against her will. Not in the bathroom, when she begged him off (then, he'd looked perplexed but not particularly miffed—"Love you, too," he'd said, and kissed her neck—which made her think he wasn't displeased, was maybe even relieved, to dodge the strained clichés of consummation), but later, in the middle of the night. Sometime between the quitting of the buses on St. James and daybreak when they started up again, she dream-felt a prodding from behind. She woke just in time to feel his first choppy thrust, and shock, more than pain, stole her breath. When she reached back, in dazed, wordless dread, to soften him, her fingers found sluglike smears of lube. For her ease or for his? She couldn't bear to ask.

"Sorry," they both blurted out, in unison, in the morning, when, jolted awake by a clang out in the hall, they jerked their stiff limbs and hit each other.

For a sec, still muzzy with sleep, she smirked at their synced apology. "Jinx!" she almost called (as she and her sister had done as kids) and counted to ten until he owed her a Coke.

But then last night's memory sank its bloody fangs in her. She turned from him and mashed her face against the starchy pillow.

She'd tried the jinx game with him once, early in their dating. During a revival-house screening of *A Place in the Sun*, they'd simultaneously whispered, "Larry Kidman," referring to the uncanny resemblance between Montgomery Clift and her new next-door neighbor. "Jinx," she chimed into the dusky theater, and he slid her a look that she could only read as pity, a stranger's wince at a spastic child's outburst.

There were so many things she did—things she'd used to do—that dating him had made her set aside. The Woody Guthrie songs she liked to belt out in the shower, imagining herself rousing a crowd of workers? "Please," he'd said, "you're from Scarsdale—a woman of the people?" She almost never ponytailed her hair anymore; he'd mentioned once it made her look "cheerleaderish." There was a kind of laughter she'd all but forgotten but would be reminded of now and then, maybe watching an *I Love Lucy* rerun all alone, when she'd hear her own fizzing giggle like the echo of a childhood nursery rhyme, and think: *Me, I remember that, that's me.*

They had so little in common. But wasn't that the excitement? Weren't those differences the magnet-pull of their love?

They *were* in love, she'd told herself whenever things got rough. This was true love, something she'd not experienced before, more contentious and painful and sometimes scarcely seeming worth it, but also deeper, so deep that if she dug out her own heart to find it, she wasn't sure she'd be able to.

Before she met him, she'd always thought of love analytically (the curse and blessing of being a scientist), as a kind of quantitative scoring system. A relationship accrued certain points for shared interests, for compatibility, for satisfaction in bed. With a tally high enough—eighty-five, say, out of a hundred—what you had qualified as love.

By this accounting, they'd failed. At virtually every level, they were lacking.

And yet. And yet.

What other than love could she call her urge to split his skull apart and wedge her own brain inside, to know everything he knew? What else was the alchemy that turned his acne scars into beauty marks, that made him say her morning breath smelled as sweet as nougat? Love, she'd found, could not be coldly counted on an abacus; it was immeasurable, a snake gulping its tail.

He was a photographer, acclaimed already, at only thirty-two, for jarringly close-up portraits of singers, dancers, senators, emphasizing every mole and pore. He had an eye for women's truths—the pith beneath the glitz—according to the photo editors (*Vogue*, *Rolling Stone*) who seemed to vie with one another to overpay him the most. The fact that he chose, when work was done, to turn that eye on her made her feel, as never before, that she was worthy of someone else's awe.

And she, gazing back at him, gave more than any model, he assured her. She was twenty-nine, a year shy of her PhD. At parties, introducing her, he often joked that they were in the same line of business, but hers was, well, a little higher-res—as if diagnostic electron microscopy were just a kind of Kodachrome on steroids.

"You see what no one else sees," he told her.

Their love was like the synesthetic trick of fireworks—not the flash or the boom or the tang of sulfur smoke but the irreducible marvel of their merging. Sometimes—say, at dinner with him—she'd shiver with a perfect chill, and it was as though love had come and plopped right down and joined them: Love, a splendid third being, beyond them.

Sometimes.

It was the other times that haunted her, when this third being, this Love, jilted them. On his birthday last August, she'd treated him to a night of favorite things: Anthony's lobster bisque, Aretha at the Orpheum. At intermission, she gave him the CD she'd special-ordered, of Aretha, as a teenager, singing gospel in church. "Scary how well you know me," he said. "This is just so perfect." They squeezed hands through the second set, their fingertips telegraphing love.

But when they boarded the T to go home, although there were any number of vacant double seats, he claimed one of the side-facing singles. He clammed up, his face erased of any seeming fondness, and she was left, bewildered, to slump in her own single seat, winded by the whack of his withdrawal. Eventually she tossed a tether—"Wasn't she great? *Three* encores?"—but he said nothing. Where had he gone? Was he a man or a hologram?

At home that night, he lay on the couch, hands behind his head, gazing up inscrutably at the ceiling. "What happened?" she asked. "Did I do something? If so, just tell me what." She knelt and brought her face close to his. "Tell me, okay? Tell me what you want." She took his hand, hoping again to feel his squeeze of love but also half wishing he might rear back and smack her. That, at least, would be contact. But he yanked back his hand and sank deeper into himself, his aqua eyes clouding, going blank.

~

In sex, he was also mystifying, hit-and-miss. At first, he wanted her all the time, in every possible way, and she, who'd never dared to truly bare herself with anyone else, cracked her hard shell of self-restraint.

She quivered unashamedly and wagged her ass in his face, grabbed his fingers and stuffed them in and taught him: *faster, faster*. How hot he was to bring her off. They blazed!

But after those initial molten sessions, his attraction cooled and hardened into a brittle, glassy coyness. He still wanted to fuck but only on his terms, which she could never fully figure out. Furtiveness seemed to fuel him, and catching her by surprise—maybe he needed to get away with something? If ever *she* tried to start things, though, he'd shrink away, sheepish, as if her interest in him was a kind of accusation.

He was fond of reaching through the curtain when she showered and tweaking her nipples until she moaned and begged him to come in. "Nah," he'd say, "I have negatives to develop."

On Valentine's Day, at Legal Seafood, he groped beneath the table and leeched his strong fingers onto her crotch. The waiter came, and he punctuated his chardonnay selection with secret pulses that beaded her brow with sweat. When the waiter left, she grabbed his wrist and whispered, "Forget dinner. Let's go fuck." His fingers, instantly limp, fell away.

Why? Why was he such a tease? What was wrong with him? (Her analytical mind couldn't rest until she solved him.)

If she had never witnessed his more open sexual self—the givingness, the gladness at their mutual appetites—maybe she could've tried to make her peace with its retreat. But she *had* seen the fuller version. She wanted to say: "I know you're more; you *want* more."

Her lab colleague, on break one day (they'd been scanning melanocytic lesions), mentioned a novel he was reading, about childhood sex abuse, the ways it eventually warped survivors. She studied him through that lens, then. Could that have happened to him? Some of his symptoms (if that was what they were) appeared to fit. Impulsiveness. Guilt. Dissociation.

And yet he could also be so perfect in sex, so present. Maybe that inconsistency itself was symptomatic?

She tried gently raising the subject, once, when they were talking about their childhoods: summer camps, oddball uncles. "Did something happen to you?" she asked.

"Happen? What do you mean?"

"When you were a kid. Did someone . . . you know. *Do* things?"

He laughed at her, a tart laugh that made her neck hairs prickle, then got up and clomped off to his darkroom.

That laugh—had it meant that she'd been miles and miles off-base? Or that she'd hit uncomfortably close to home? If the latter, how could she fault him, or risk compounding his wound? She wanted to help, to heal. If only he would let her.

What bad thing had happened to *her*—always so rational otherwise—that she would choose to martyr herself like this? No trauma in her girlhood, no dearth of any kind. Loving parents, a sheltered suburb, every imaginable privilege. Except, for her, that very privilege had pressed her out of shape. Goaded her and shamed her. *To whom much is given . . .*

Nice theory, she told herself, but maybe a total crock. More likely there was no accounting for why she was so drawn to him—or maybe the lack of an explanation *was* what drew her in: for once in her life, a problem she couldn't fix, or even diagnose, no matter how well her view was magnified. A constant unanswerable itch. An addiction.

~

She tried to quit. Just once, when his blankness grew too bleak and she feared he might never reemerge. It was a week after their fizzled Valentine's dinner, and since then he had hardly looked her in the face. She made a show of taking a pillow and blanket to the couch, and told him, "Sorry. Not sure I can do this anymore."

"This?" he said.

"Your disappearing act."

He shook his head, and shrugged, and shuffled up the stairs.

The next day, she came home from a workout, hamstrings humming, ready for a long Epsom bath. He ambushed her in the hallway. Stripped away her sweats. They did it without speaking—without even breathing, was how it seemed. Her hips jammed the wainscoting, her head knocked plaster dust from the wall, but she could feel no pain, only geysering relief. *Here* he was! Here. Right inside her.

Crazy, said a distant, deadened voice within her chest. Am I the kind of woman so dependent, so unfinished, that a cock is all I need to keep me hooked?

But no, what connected them went deeper, so much deeper.

He hugged her hips and acrobatically brought her to the floor, managing somehow still to stay inside her. "Thank you," he said. "I know it's hard. I do. I know I'm not . . ."

He stared at her, not like a photographer snapping a portrait but like a pilgrim arriving at a shrine. She stared back, imagining she could see clear through to his retinas—way, way back, among the rods and cones—certain that his love for her, and her uncommon love for him, was too essential ever to dissolve.

~

"God, how tacky," he said.

They were in Fenway Park, watching the Sox get slaughtered by the Twins. She downed a nugget of Cracker Jack and followed his pointed finger to the sky. Above the bleachers puttered a biplane, trailing a big red banner: MARRY ME.

"Tacky?" she said. "I think it's super romantic."

He grinned. "Yeah, I knew that's what you'd say. That's why I did it."

"Wait," she said. "You don't mean . . . ?"

Just then the Wave reached their section of the grandstand; his yes drowned in a melee of hurrahs.

Yes, she said, too. The whole crowd was watching. How could she have answered anything else?

She worried, though. Was she dooming herself to a lifetime on a knife's edge? To an endlessly exhausting ambiguity? Or worse, maybe: What if marriage erased that ambiguity? What if he'd feel permission now to disappear more often, to stop always re-earning her attachment?

His own best friend, Tom, had once offered a warning: "I love the guy, but the worst thing you can do for him is a favor. Makes him take you all the more for granted."

But yes, she'd said. Yes. She stuck with it.

She stuck with it, imagining—hoping—that her yes might finally heal whatever injury had lamed him. A cure as enigmatic as the wound. The force of law and history, of such a public commitment: maybe marriage was something you couldn't fathom until you lived it.

~

The planning worked wonders. Whenever they started shouldering their rifles of resentment, there were other foes at whom to aim: their parents, all of a sudden dogmatically nostalgic, who yearned to hijack the ceremony to replicate their own; the fish-resistant caterer; the ABBA-phobic DJ; the rabbi, allegedly liberal, who balked at every inching from tradition. Pitted against this onslaught, they bonded like convicts on the lam. At the florist's, viewing centerpieces, he softly kissed her ear. "Pick whichever," he said. "I want what you do." He turned down a fashion shoot to whisk her to Nantucket, where they cuddled in the beach-plum-scented dunes.

At such moments, blinking past the snags of a big event, she couldn't help but believe she was glimpsing their lighter future. Like dry ice sublimating directly into vapor, they'd find themselves, once married, transmuted into something else entirely: husband and wife.

(Had she succumbed to the make-believe of the wedding-industrial complex? Swallowed the barb hidden in its bait? But no, if she knew that risk and guarded herself against it, and *still* she felt such hope? Must be real.)

Scanning the Bible for a verse they and the rabbi could agree on, they came upon a quote from Ecclesiastes: "Two are better than one, because they have a good reward for their toil. For if they fall, one will lift up the other; but woe to one who is alone and falls and does not have another to help." This was perfect: it was just how they'd met! On the Green Line one Friday night, riding to her friend's monthly potluck, she'd let go of the commuter strap in order to crimp the tin foil on her quiche. The train curved into Boylston; lurching, it jerked her forward. Her idiotic instinct: save the quiche! She tumbled, both hands holding it tight, nothing to break her fall. Except him. There he was, this stranger, all six feet two of him, with able arms that seemed designed expressly to hold her up. After she regained her feet, they introduced themselves. By Coolidge Corner, he'd agreed to join her at the potluck, the "feel free to bring a guest" she'd never brought before. Two months later, they moved in together. "We fell in love," she told everyone, "literally."

They found the Bible verse in the middle of a Tuesday, which they'd taken off to tie up the liturgy's last loose ends. They were so tickled by its appropriateness, and by the memory of their serendipitous meeting, that right then, even with the sun slicing in through open curtains and their actions on display for any passerby, they stripped their pants and fucked, standing up. Who had started it, he or she? Neither. Both at once. It felt as though they'd never *not* been moving like this, together. Skin and breath and marrow sweetly burning.

Even this, she thought. Even sex, especially sex. Marriage will give us everything in common.

~

The ceremony was flawless. Or, rather, it was the kind of magical event in which even the mishaps came off as triumphs. And so, when the white-rose garland failed to arrive, her sister discovered violets blooming in the courtyard; in minutes she had woven a dazzling wreath. And when the trumpeters missed their cue for the processional, and she waited what seemed forever at the door, the silence amplified her like a spotlight. In that hush as all the guests turned to her—no sound but the whisper of women's dresses—she heard the new, quicker syncopation of her heart, which now would join eternally with his.

He looked real in his crisp black tuxedo. That was the word that occurred to her, that here, at last, this was the *real* him. He'd had his hair cut: blunt, candid bangs.

The rabbi recited the blessings, the Ecclesiastes passage. They traded rings, then each sipped from the same cup of wine: tiny gestures, but bigger than the scope of both their lives until just now.

After their kiss, giddy, they almost walked away, but the rabbi stopped them, lifting up an empty champagne flute. He swaddled it, babylike, in a pink linen cloth, and placed the small package at their feet. Conventionally, crushing the glass was the new husband's task, but they had chosen to do it together—everything from now on would be together. She placed her shoe on top of his; they stomped.

They hardly spoke during the reception, busy making the rounds of relatives. But across the thronged room they kept catching each other's eyes and smiling a new private married smile. When the band played "Time after Time," they danced so close she felt his neck's pulse.

After the cake was cut, his aunt organized the chair dance. With stomach-curdling thrill, she was lifted above the crowd. She clutched her chair with one hand, and with the other gripped a scarf, the opposite end of which, from his hoisted chair, he held. The aunt led the customary cheer: "Siman tov u'mazal tov, u'mazal tov v'siman tov." But the younger generation overcame her: "Cinnamon toast and Melba toast, and Melba toast and cinnamon toast." So amused were the revelers by their silly sacrilege, they neglected to stabilize the chairs. She teetered, trying to counterbalance, unable to grasp his hand directly but clinging to the flimsy scarf that joined them. Suddenly they were sprawled on the ground, gasping for breath, addled. Her ears rang. She managed, still, to smile.

"Yes, we've all heard," her sister deadpanned. "You *fell* in love."

A few more taxing dances, the last cheek-straining photos, and soon they were riding in the limo to the Copley, and then up the elevator to the swank honeymoon suite. A touch drunk, she shucked her dress and stumbled into the bathroom, eager to take out her gritty contacts.

He came to her and teased her nipples, but she was in a new mood now. Placid, already gratified. What was the rush? What did she have to prove?

"Later," she said, and kissed him, and off they went to bed. She dropped into a sleep as thick as tar.

Noise in the hotel hallway: a metal clang, a curse. Jolted awake, they thrashed and smacked each other.

"Sorry," they both blurted, at exactly the same time.

"Jinx!" she almost called, but the ache was suddenly everywhere. Rawness where he'd rammed her in the middle of the night, and also in her throat, a jagged laceration where her tries to say "Stop!" had got stuck.

Staggered silent, scared, she'd reached back to tame him. "Don't," he'd said, and grabbed her wrist. "Don't," until he finished. In seconds, he was stomach-down and snoring.

An hour or more, she'd lain there, trying to calm her shakes. Trying not to feel the coming bruises.

Then the buses, huffing past below, on St. James—spewing a haze she knew she couldn't smell but thought she might. A snuffing smog that knocked her back into the muck of sleep.

And now, snapped awake by the crash out in the hall, she looked at him, ready to accuse. But he had turned away and was already fast asleep again, his chest easy, in and out with breath.

She twisted her new ring around, then halfway round again, the diamond pointing in, toward her palm. We fell in love, she reminded herself. Her fist clenched the splinter-sharp gem.

Marge

Marge had long blond ringlets and eyes like poached eggs. He only ever wanted to be a housewife: the slippers, the curlers in his hair. Plus, I think he maybe craved an accent. He talked like he was trying to keep from downing a bite of mush.

Also, I suppose, he'd have liked to be called "she." But this was the '80s. We weren't ready for that. At least, I wasn't.

His mother had won the lottery years back and bought a building with ten rental units Marge could manage. Pronto he hired a crew, turned the ten into twenty-five—so measly, folks said, that if you sneezed in one apartment, everyone God-blessed you in the next.

Marge rented mostly to whores—or, really, to their pimps. The first of the month he slippered through the halls: Pay-up time, would come his porridge voice. The pimps just beat him up. What could he do about it?

Whenever he made a peep, they sent in punks to fuck with him: arrange his plastic plates across his stove and light the burners. The next day, he'd chip the hardened plastic from the stove, then hustle off to Goodwill to buy new plastic plates. Ah, he'd say with put-on cheer, the landlady's life!

I guess he felt he didn't exactly own the moral high ground. He liked young boys: twelve, thirteen, fourteen. (He himself, no matter the year, was always not quite thirty.) The whores and I would sit downstairs and watch the boys go in, then watch them come out twenty minutes later.

If a kid left with a Hershey's kiss in addition to his cash, it meant he'd been very, very good. A tangerine or a gumball, only so-so.

I want to die smiling, Marge said. Boys make me happy.

Sometimes a boy gave me his tangerine as he left. Maybe he knew he'd been a disappointment. He'd ask if that dude's name was really Marge. Someone would say sure, course it was. It might not have been the name Marge got from his mother. How much truth do our mothers ever give?

I lived with mine, supposedly, in the building next door, but mostly I was left to my own self. Mom worked for one of the guys who clobbered Marge on rent days. My pops was dead, or might as well have been.

One day I was cutting school, ants were in my pants. Hotter than it should've been for June. How would I manage—crank a hydrant, maybe? Suck some ice? I shuffled down to the street in my boxers, nothing else. Sunlight sharp and dogged as an itch. There was Marge, lounging on his stoop, next to ours: flimsy housedress, hair pulled back and tied. It made his face look big, a flexed muscle.

Out from Marge's robe came a leg as long as lightning. Now I saw the bowl, the shaving cream. He used a Lady Schick, just like Mom's. Stroke, stroke—one leg, then the next—stroke, like harvesting a crop. His skin got pearly, catching all the light. I peered into the rinse bowl: sprinkled hairs, all those zillion tiny twists of fate. It felt like the legs he stroked were mine.

I'd shave you, too, he said. His voice made me sizzle. But your thingy? It's really more a *toe* than a leg, ain't it?

He pointed down. It poked clear through my fly.

I ran inside, locked the door, and panted prayers to God. Begged Him not to let me be like Marge.

~

Thirty-some years on, our hood has gotten chic. Bargain hunters troll the streets with ponytailed Realtors who chatter about *vested interest, upswing*. They're as slim and glassy as the iPhones they whip out to call their mortgage brokers and say, Buy. Way back then, we could've used those cells. One day Ma Bell came and yanked the public pay phones—

stripped for coins too often to be worth it. Mom couldn't afford a private number. Now, how would she ever call for help?

We were natives waiting for our continent to be plundered. Street signs said NO STANDING, so we sat. Best seats in the house for Marge's show: at last, would Marge discover true love?

Merge was what I dubbed him in my mind—part one thing, part another, all mixed up. But the pimps called him Marge of Dimes, grand marshal of the freak parade.

He raised his chin and tried to make light of all his bruises, naming them with catalog-type terms. Strife, he called a certain purple shade just shy of black. Yellow tinged with blue: Mottled Remorse.

Looking back, I think of him as Marginalia. His endless commentating made life almost graspable. Prodigious! he might say of a scorching August noon. Hot as the hole of an overtime ho! He evangelized his own low-down church. Jesus and the Holy Rolling three-way, he once barked at a B-boy who wouldn't mind his paws. I'll whup your ass to dingleberry jam!

Most everything reminded Marge of food. The moles on a preteen Puerto Rican beauty's cheek were currants in a bowl of oatmeal. An uppity cholo's backside was his tasty hot cross bun. (Lick it, Marge advised, during Lent.) Once, fifteen feet before I turned onto our block, I heard him diss someone's face as *tragically shapeless*. God must've forgot to heat his griddle, Marge continued, before he poured in *that* bit of batter. From the way he got cackling when I cornered into view, I figured he was talking about me.

Too old for him already, I guessed, my upper lip fuzzed with linty hair. In two years, I had grown ten luckless inches. A tall drink of juice, he told me once.

I was a boy-watcher, too, but kept my comments silent. I studied how they strutted, how they pop-'n'-locked, the way they picked their hair but not too much. I snuck enough peeks to crib their moves.

The juice was in my privates. Did Marge know?

I learned people like all sorts of things. One bald grandad happily parted with two Franklins weekly for Mom to twiddle her thumbs up in his ass. Another man—she called him Reagan, rich and overtanned—

wanted fishing weights hung from his nipples. All manner of noises came from next door. People craved whatever they craved, did what it took to get it.

Except for me. My itch for Marge? I couldn't.

Where did he find the guys who would? The Y, maybe. The chop shop by the river. I envied them: their ballsiness, their finders-keepers pleasure.

In some more polished neighborhood, or some more polished town, people marched and waved their rainbow flags and begged for rights. They'd have hated Marge, I think, even more than they loathed the guys who beat him. The last thing Marge wanted was to be "just like you."

The plate-melting punks asked me along once: Damon, whose honey-smooth moonwalk made me hungry; Pedro, with the big bulge in his track pants. It was Halloween. The air reeked of cornstalks and other dried-up country stuff. The stink of plastic jack-o'-lanterns singeing.

Shaving cream was part of the night's plan, and rotten eggs. A can of Crisco, too—who knew why? This would be my chance, I thought, to look close-up at Marge's life. My chance to prove what I didn't want.

I'd been in his building before, but now it felt a shade of unfamiliar. The light was like a stain on normal light. Behind a hollow door, someone's hand slapped someone's something. I heard: Feels good. And: No the fuck you don't.

SWAT-style, we slithered up the stairs, down the hall, rotten-egg grenades set for launching. We got to Marge's door, and Damon karate-kicked it. In we blitzed, screaming skinned-alive.

It took a sec to focus, to see beyond our bluster. Marge was in his clawfoot tub, knitting. Something pink and cabled, maybe a baby blanket. He might've had a niece we didn't know.

The room was frilly, chockablock with lace and fake flowers. Flesh-colored candles like dildos on all the shelves. Foil-wrapped kisses in pink plastic bowls. You know how, when you're sick, the best relief is puking? I wanted to spit up my whole self.

Trick or treat, called Damon, with bug-out goblin eyes.

Nah, corrected Pedro. Dickless freak! He hawked hard and spat into the bath.

Marge just kept on knitting. Locked his jaw.

Faggot, Damon said. You a man, or what the fuck? Stand the fuck up, show us what you got.

Yeah, I said, wanting the guys to think I shared their toughness. Plus, because I hoped to catch a glimpse.

Damon cocked his fist. Hear me? Up!

Marge grimaced. Knit one, purl two.

The bubble bath's fruity smell was killing us with kindness.

Let's fuckin' stomp him, Pedro said.

Damon's arm stayed cocked but didn't move. Above his elbow's inside hinge, a tiny pulse showed. It fluttered. He wasn't yet fifteen.

Fuck 'im, he said. Her. Whatever the fuck: it. I hate the way it won't quit *lookin'* at me.

We're just giving it its jollies, added Pedro.

They scrammed, spurting foam across the walls, on the bed. Damon hurled the Crisco at a lightbulb-bordered mirror. Two bulbs popped like back talk: *yap, yap*.

Ready . . . aim . . . , yelled Pedro.

On *fire* they launched their rotten eggs. I chucked mine, too, a wicked sidearm fling.

The way you see a lightning bolt before you hear the crack, at first I watched the yolk ooze down in streaks. All three scored: Marge's jaw, above each of his eyes. Pretty in a certain way, like drippy abstract art. Then *boom!* came the thunder of the smell. A death stink. Abortions, gangrene.

Get the fuck—Marge yelled, then caught himself.

The yolks' yellow clashed on the pink of baby blanket. Red, then, too: blood across his brow. I guess his skin wasn't especially thick, after all.

The other guys hoofed it to the hall, and I followed. But when I hit the threshold, I halted. My brain blazed: a hot coal that Marge's gaze was fanning.

I turned back and found one of his fluffy bath towels, as soft as my grandmother's cheek. (Bullshit! I never met either of my grandmothers.) I stepped up and handed it to him.

Closer, here, inside the smell, it wasn't quite so bad. Nasty still, but flowery too, perfumed. Marge had his left eye half-closed like a wink, which made him seem forgiving, even charmed. Slimy white stuff dripped along his cheek.

Much obliged, he said in a posh, tea-party voice, and dabbed the towel suavely on his brow. Then he started to rise, and the foamy bubbles parted. He stood facing me. His skin shone.

For the first time, I understood that shameless wasn't bad, but maybe an ideal, an aspiration. Marge was so much taller than I had thought. His hair down there was reddish—the parts he hadn't shaved. His thing curved like a smirk. It looked like mine.

I sprinted out and told the other guys the freak had grabbed me. Shit, I said, he's stronger than he looks.

~

I waited for Marge to say something. Waited a day, a week. What I wanted: to never see his fuckhead face again. What I wanted: assurance, an invitation.

His boys came and went (Marge joked: Came, came, and went). I searched their faces. Triumph? Resignation? They had a talent or a recklessness I lacked.

The country reelected an old actor. Plus, there was a referendum on a new subway line, to maybe, at last, extend the tracks out to where we lived. The verdict? Wouldn't kill us to keep walking.

Clementine season came: for weeks that's what the so-so boys departed Marge's with. One kid, with freckles and a harelip, gave me his. Sick, I said, and threw it at his skinny ass. I missed.

Marge, running low on his supply of willing boys, had to make do with grown men. Their moods were iffy, harder, their knuckles harder, too. New shades of bruise were soon coined. Misdemeanor (grayish). Loss of Face.

For Christmas, Mom wowed me with a leather basketball, too nice to dribble on blacktop. I kept it mint in the box: a wish that hadn't yet been disappointed. Mom split for a week with Miguel, the guy who kept her. Reno, she said—so they could tie the knot. (What she tied, really, was her tubes.) That week I ate SpaghettiOs and whacked off.

My body was like a TV that someone was channel-surfing: now sweat, now hormones, now hair, *click-click-click*. Everything was new, up for grabs.

Pedro and Damon formed a gang. *Which side are you on?* With heated pins and ballpoint ink, they tattooed their right forearms: a time bomb with a clock face that read SOON.

Fools, said Marge. You really gonna *choose* to fuck your skin up? (His own latest unchosen laceration had barely healed.)

I took his advice, resisted. Hoped he'd see from my rolled-up sleeves that I was more loyal to him than to Damon.

If Marge noticed, he didn't give a damn. I'd stood in his apartment, face to face, seen his all. I'd almost apologized, almost begged. But that moment, so monumental to me, for him was nothing. Battered and bare was Marge's every night.

Chickenshit, said Damon finally, grabbing my virgin arm. He twisted an Indian burn. Thrilling pain.

Do it, I said.

Ink me, I said.

I'm in.

~

In February, I tailed one of the chocolate-kiss boys. I'd seen him around school but didn't know him. He was a mix, his skin the brown of our rusted window grates, and whetstone-gray eyes that sharpened you.

He was maybe sixteen. Me too, nearly.

Leaving Marge's, he swaggered with an extra fuck in his stride, tossing and catching his silver kiss like a coin. The braces on his teeth yanked in sunlight when he grinned. With each step, he kicked his own future.

I followed him down Washington, then behind the Laundromat—an alley that was Bomb Squad turf. The week before, Pedro and I had bopped a kid back there, a smart-mouth who called us fucking cretins. All we'd shaken loose was a pack of Camel Lights, but his cheek against my fist? Totally worth it. Recently we'd also lifted forties from Cappy's Liquor. We practiced pickpocketing each other. Damon talked big about going back to Marge's and nailing him this time, no retreat. My tattoo was the color of a vein.

A rat in the alley nosed a Zero bar wrapper. A broken mirror cut the sky to bits. The kid—couldn't think of his name, but he looked like a Leon—bent and fished fivers from his sock. Counting, maybe. Maybe glorifying.

His money wasn't what I was after. But how do you ask for what you really want? I gunned my hand and jabbed him. Fork it over!

Leon didn't flinch. A headband kept his curls off his eyes.

Now! I said. Give it up, cocksucker.

Leon just stuffed the cash back into his sock. He stood straight up. I was tall, but he was taller. Thick.

I hadn't really thought things through this far. Tail the kid, get close to him . . . then what?

I know where you've been, I sort of croaked.

He snorted and said, You don't know shit. Half of his mouth smiled, but the other half stayed mean. His braces looked made of razor wire.

Laundry steam hovered like something consequential. I thought about skedaddling but couldn't. I was trying to picture him, his body, in Marge's bath. What I wanted to ask: *How's it feel?*

He grabbed my arm, his thumb on the double *o* of SOON, and pressed like he was digging clear to China—to the opposite of this place we were stuck in. Now I remembered his father coached the b-ball team at school, and his name wasn't Leon, it was Darrell. Darrell was the youngest but the best varsity player. A power forward. All-city. Eyed by scouts.

I want, he said—then paused long enough for me to wonder—I want to hear it come out of your mouth.

What?

That you don't know shit.

You're right, I said. I don't. Let me go.

He tippy-toed nearer, his mouth up in my face. I saw a smear of Hershey's on his teeth. His breath was like the Y locker room at closing time: bleach trying to hide a human stink. I made a guess about what he had swallowed.

Don't what? made a breeze that kissed my chin. He gripped me harder.

Don't know shit, I said. Okay? I don't know anything.

The anger in his eyes was so fierce I almost heard it, the *shick-shick* of steel being edged.

I'm not what you think I am, he said. Or what you are.

I could feel my flesh giving under his thumb's pressure. When the bruise rose, what would I name its hue?

Darrell said, I'm gettin' the fuck out. I'm gonna make it. Is you or anyone gonna mess with that?

No one, I said.

He knocked me to the ground.

~

The next day was Friday. I was loafing, out on the stoop, tiddleywinking bottle caps. Miguel was there, and Mom, too, bra cups stuffed with cash. Alley drafts tickled at our ears.

Thank God for the weekend, said Miguel. He cracked his knuckles.

Nah, thank God there *ain't* no God, Mom was quick to sass. Otherwise I'd meet you shits in hell!

Laughter all around. High fives.

Damon and Pedro had cooked up a little Bomb Squad mischief: a rooftop, a case of beer, some girls. I wanted time to shower, clean my teeth.

Just as I stood up, I saw a flash of silver fang and someone's scissor stride. Darrell, headband skewed, bolting from Marge's building. Darrell, both hands empty at his sides.

Mom snickered. That one of Marge's boys?

Must've been a dud, said Miguel. Where's his chocolate?

You never know, said Mom. Might be in his pocket. Boys do hide their treasures in their pants.

They chuckled, but I couldn't. Already I was scrambling—into Marge's building, up the stairs. The door was open. Fruity smells leaked out.

I stepped inside. I blinked hard. I looked.

Thirty years later, I still see it. I see that scene more clearly than my high school graduation, more clearly than the day I finished Rutgers—the first diplomas in my family. It's sharper than my wedding, six years later, to Teresa, whose hair, when it's damp, curls like Marge's. (Sometimes when we're fucking, I twist some on my finger, and Terri has no notion what I'm thinking.) It's clearer to me, now, than this screen I'm typing on.

Shards of pink plastic bowl were scattered on the floor, half a dozen chocolates smeared around. Centered in the midst of it lay Marge: blond ringlets strewn about like sunlight in fast water, cotton robe bunched around his hips.

His mouth, stretched past normal, was crammed with chocolate kisses. A dozen? Two? Maybe more. Most still in their foil, some smushed out.

Thumbprints on his neck. Breath and pulse both gone. Already his skin was turning gray.

On cop shows, they're always saying not to move the body. Don't touch a thing. Call 911.

You think the cops would've rushed for Marge?

I straightened out the robe so his legs were mostly covered. Arranged his ringlets nice around his face. Then, with my finger, I dug into his mouth to clear away the mushy, melting chocolate. Sickening at first—giblets out of a chicken—but then it started to feel not so bad, then almost good.

When all the smashed kisses I could reach were emptied out, I saw his mouth—*her* mouth—had fallen to a smile. I tried hard to smile back but couldn't. I faced a long lifetime of restraint.

Backing away, I stumbled. My hand went to my face. An accident, an instinct: I slipped my finger into my mouth. Have I ever tasted anything as sweet?

The Gift of Travel

Jim kept saying he wanted to take a last-blast trip together. His treat, just the two of us—my first chance to venture beyond New England. He was in hock to hospitals in Maine and Massachusetts, he'd maxed out his credit cards on smuggled Mexican meds, but he was sitting on ninety-seven thousand Delta miles: enough to take us somewhere with a strong, restoring sun. He'd hoarded the miles in the past few years, before he got too sick to fly, hopping from campus to campus with his retrospective lecture "Filthy as Fuck: A Faggot Writer's Life." This was 1993; in the newly rising queer studies programs at Duke, Yale, et al., suddenly it was in to be outrageous.

Did Jim truly think the trip was anything but a pipe dream? Think that he could clamber out of his frailness, back to passable health, and someday might jet away again? Probably not, but keep in mind, his forte was erotica—his plots, like most of their genre, adamantly implausible. "Know what you need to make it in this business?" he'd asked me once. "Anyone can describe a thrusting, pulsing blah blah blah. The tougher thing to do is suspension of disbelief. Wishful thinking—*that's* the secret weapon."

When I would play along with Jim's vision of a trip, I wasn't exactly trying to humor him. More like trying to buffer him from the truth. (I hadn't yet wondered if he was trying to buffer me.)

"Picture it, Ben," he mused one day as I prepared to flush his Hickman catheter. "Copacabana at sunset. My wise and worldly cock inside your twinky little bum."

"Sure," I said, swabbing the lumen's end with alcohol. "Sounds delicious. All except the last part."

"Ouch!" he cried.

The catheter site was purplish and crepey. Had I stung Jim's skin or his pride? Even by then, as close as we were, I had trouble finding the line between his jokes and his joke-barnacled vulnerability.

"Still so stingy, Ben?" he said. "*Still?* When I'm *dying*? Jesus, don't you want me to die happy?"

"I want for you not to die," I said, but maybe he didn't hear me, seeing as he was only partway through his giddy tantrum.

"Tell me this isn't about your pledge to Thomas," he said. "Saint Thomas! Martyr for the cause of monogamy."

Thomas was my boyfriend—or *had* been, for five-plus years, since we were college freshmen. Nine and a half weeks ago, he'd moved to San Francisco to take a wetlands restoration position at Point Reyes. But really, to put a continent between us. A trial separation, while Thomas considered my bid to win him back.

"No?" said Jim. "Ah, I see. It's *me*."

Then "Ma," he barked, turning to Betty, who sat in the bedside armchair. "Ma, can you believe this kid's cruelty?"

His mother eyed him over her bifocals. "Oh, Jimmy," she said, her voice plump with disapproval, as though he'd asked for a second bowl of pudding. Then this Daughter of the American Revolution; this Republican former librarian of Brockton, Massachusetts; this rock-ribbed, churchy-voiced, octogenarian widow said, "Leave him be, for heaven's sake. He doesn't want your cock."

Betty was right. But the problem wasn't that Jim was dying or what he was dying of; I hadn't wanted him even before the AIDS had gone full-blown. Nor was it that he was unalluring. When he was healthy, Jim had had a thrillingly hard handsomeness—the kind of aristocratic face you'd see in a castle's statuary—and even now, eroded to the essence of himself, even now he sizzled with charisma. His pebbly eyes, the plow blades of his jaw. Who could resist the scrumptious clash between his courtly looks and his smutty disposition?

I could, apparently.

Jim had published a story of mine in one of his anthologies, a show of faith in a fresh-from-college writer. This led to flirty postcards, then a phone friendship (he lived in Portland, Maine; I in Boston), and finally to his hiring me as a mostly long-distance assistant. I answered correspondence, managed his speaking gigs, and, as his powers waned and deadlines started slipping, increasingly ghostwrote his works in progress: his tale of stranded astronauts who fall in frenzied love; *Dave and Jon*, his bawdy biblical update.

I had told him, early on, when he said he "had" to fuck me ("You're my protégé, that's the protocol"), that I thought it was better if we kept our bond professional. Except the word I fumbled for was *clean*. "A dirty fag writer and you want to keep things clean?" he'd said. "I'm not sure you're even teachable."

Whenever I'd mentioned Thomas—our snug equilibrium, which I'd had no intention (until I did it) of upsetting—Jim would rant about our prudish, thankless generation. "*This* is why we marched? And screamed our fucking faces off? And sat in all those nasty jail cells—*this*? For your right to be such boring marrieds?"

I loved those rants, actually, wowed to sit at the feet of a man who'd lived through—who'd *made*—such big swaths of history. He'd been a hustler, a towel boy at the Continental Baths, a correspondent for *Gay Community News*. In 1970, after the notorious Snake Pit raid, when one of the men arrested leapt from the precinct's second story, impaling himself on a spiked metal fence, Jim had helped to organize the protest.

He had been *there*: "there" being a past I longed to touch, and also a feeling of life as large and urgent.

I loved his self-certainty, his hunger for the world, his cheerfully lewd, give-no-fucks affections. He was like the socket to a source of thrumming voltage—everything I was eager to plug into—so why, then? Why had I resisted?

He was my mentor; I wanted him to want me for my writing.

Plus, wouldn't our sleeping together have seemed too neatly plotted? The sort of cliché that Jim's own work was sometimes faulted for?

But no, those are literary excuses, invented later. In truth, at twenty-three—my body smooth and slinky, my hair a potent shock of baby blond—I simply couldn't fathom sex with any man as old as Jim, even if being sexy was his profession.

Forty-six. A year younger than I am now.

The Hickman line delivered Jim's nutrition intravenously and had to be flushed with heparin daily to keep his blood from clotting. I screwed the syringe into the lumen and opened the catheter clamp. Weeks ago, when the nurse had trained me, I'd been tense with fear—less of Jim's infected blood than of the chance I'd kill him with an accidental bubble—but now, as I firmly pushed the plunger with my thumb, shooting the clear liquid toward his heart, my body throbbed with a proud, awestruck sense of competence.

When all the hep was injected and I'd reclamped the catheter, I tried to read Jim's face for signs of nausea. (Sometimes the flushing gagged him with a rancid-garlic scent, though I'd smell only alcohol's bleak sting.) But Jim appeared at ease. In fact, he was snoozing—lately he could drop asleep in the middle of a sentence. Beside him, Betty, too, had seemingly nodded off; a fat mass-market spy novel was falling from her lap.

I sat there, in the gloam of Jim's cloyingly stale apartment, amazed by how unamazed I was. He was the first person with AIDS I'd ever helped to care for, and when I'd started, a year ago, I had expected stink and gore and sobs. But sometimes it was only this: a silent, sleepy room.

Padding to the trash can with the used syringe and swabs, I was jarred by a ghoulish, hissing voice—had it said "Sorry"? I spun around, and there was Jim, devilishly grinning.

"Sorry," he hissed again, then loosed a death's-head cackle. "You'll be sorry you never let me fuck you."

~

That was before the thrush that left him fighting to swallow his spit, before the seizure (a mini stroke? toxoplasmosis?) that froze him on the couch, only his eyes alive, when I could think of nothing to do but light a Merit and hold it to his lips as we awaited the paramedics.

Three months later, we understood he'd never leave his room again. He'd made me and his mother promise: No hospital. No medicine, except to ease his end. The Casco Bay breeze we cracked the windows to let in was the closest he could come now to adventure.

It was hard to watch his world shrink to just this. He was a man of boundless nerve, of cornucopian passions, who claimed to have spilled his seed on every single continent. (Well, if you counted a Princess cruise ship, anchored off Antarctica.) For me, raised by a pair of wary, small-town sticks-in-the-mud, Jim was like a mind-expanding drug. My parents seemed to revel in their limited horizons, their mindset best summed up by my father's favorite T-shirt, an ad for our local hardware store: "If we don't have it, you don't need it." But Jim recoiled at any inhibition. Once, when he'd caught the whiff of minimalism in a story of mine, he red-inked in the margin, "*More* is more!" He was bent on reaming my psyche clean of its old clogs.

Or had been, before he took to bed.

As he had gotten sicker, I'd been going to Portland more often, trading nursely duties with his mother and with Dean, an eighteen-year-old florist's helper Jim had cottoned to. Dean asked me if I could come one Friday night in April—he had lined up a dinner date with some unlikely prospect, a lobster packer with hands, he said, "as big as waffle irons"—and I was happy to rearrange my shifts. At Glad Day, the gay bookstore where I was underpaid counter help, Friday nights were even more insanely cruisy than normal, and, since I was trying to prove myself again to Thomas—no more hookups with anyone, I'd pledged—it was a good time to get away.

I headed north in my chattery, Nixon-era Chevy Nova, babying the balky transmission. (I'd bought it from a pal of my boss's—a hundred and fifty bucks—when I had started making these trips to Maine.) Past the tacky, towering, hilltop eateries on Route 1, the mattress stores and by-the-hour motels, and finally onto the buzzing, burnished span of interstate. Spring was just a faint fuzz of yellow-green potential, a blur along the stark, still-bare trees. I had the radio on, and when Whitney Houston started belting "I Will Always Love You," I let myself grow soaringly sentimental. I'd called Thomas the night before, late even for him, on San Francisco time. His voice—its chronic frogginess, its modest swallowed *r*'s—consoled me as no one else's could. We had talked for nearly an hour. Or mostly *not* talked, actually, but just let a loose silence bind us.

At one point, when neither of us had spoken for a minute, he broke the hush with "So, how are your nips?" This was our oldest inside joke, a reference to the marathon he'd run our first April. Cheerleader-in-chief, I'd waited at the top of Heartbreak Hill—more than twenty miles into the race—with energy bars, bananas, a jar of Vaseline. When Thomas approached, blind with fatigue, I hollered, "How are your nips?" He staggered over, lifting his sweaty singlet, and the crowd went wild as I smeared Vaseline across his nipples.

"They'd be better," I'd said last night, "if you were here to lick 'em." I waited to see if he'd play along. He didn't. "Hey, it's just a week till this year's marathon," I said. I told him about the cusp-of-spring air now kissing Boston. "Miss it?" I asked. "In Frisco, do they even *have* seasons?"

"Know what I miss? Maybe this sounds kooky," Thomas said. "I miss it when the last snow melts, and suddenly you can smell all the dog poo."

"Seriously?"

"Yeah, I always found it, I don't know, reassuring. The way things thaw? Such an honest smell."

Oh, what a quintessentially Thomas-y response! He himself had often smelled of the natural world he worked in: salty and wet and green, elemental. He would come home and cloak me in that sodden, comfy scent. He'd also bring bouquets he'd gathered: maidenhair ferns, cattails. Careful to avoid anything that might set off my allergies. Always careful, and always full of care.

How, then, could I have been so uncaring to him?

Until he'd left, I couldn't have conceived of his ever leaving. Steady Thomas, whose version of a big change, before, was showing up at Sully's for his Tuesday burgers-and-bingo night and ordering medium rare instead of medium.

Now he'd been gone for almost half a year.

"What else do you miss?" I asked, unabashedly fishing. These past months without him—without sex at all—had left me in a wobbly dark, as though, this whole time, I'd been pinching shut my eyes. It would all be worth it, I hoped: how brightly, when I finally looked again, the world would gleam.

"I miss not being mad at you," said Thomas.

It hurt to hear him say that, but his tone was soft, pensive, not the stiff scolding I'd grown used to. A measure of progress, or so I wanted to think.

By the time we hung up—after more loose silence—I was lost in picturing San Francisco: curls of fog, sun on cresting whitecaps. Maybe after . . . after Jim . . . I couldn't name the word. But soon, when my nursing duties here would not be needed, I could join Thomas in California.

The speeding cars on I-95 rushed at me like predators, but then, as if my old, decaying Nova killed their appetites, angled to my left and hurtled past. I gave the car gas, the engine cleared its throat, and on we juddered across the state line. Here was the famous billboard, which struck me now less as an invitation than a taunt: WELCOME TO MAINE: THE WAY LIFE SHOULD BE.

Why had I cheated? Why? That was what Thomas had pressed to know, but I had not been able yet to reckon with an answer. I hadn't been aware of feeling unfulfilled by him, or felt I'd been chafing against chains. Our sex, even after all these years, could be rambunctious. I found Thomas's broody eyes and his big, boxy jaw more elegant with every passing day.

We'd met at Salem State, in Lit I, two greenhorn gay boys, fresh off the boat from our grim hetero homelands. (I was from Dracut, a town exactly as charming as its name, my mom a cashier at Cumby's, my dad an HVAC sales rep; Thomas's parents were postal clerks from Methuen, the next town over.) As refugees, together we embraced our queer new culture—its sly lingo and upside-down styles—but also offered each other a haven of the familiar. Monogamy wasn't a principle we'd ever quite agreed to; no other choice would've occurred to us.

For years, when Thomas had badmouthed the notion of sex with strangers ("What's the point of pleasing some guy you'll never see again?"), I had always reflexively agreed. For us, sex was never an end in itself but just a means, a way to buttress the love we built together. After school, when we moved to Boston and I found work at Glad Day, I got my first close-up view of the anonymous hookup scene. I watched the men who scuffled around the porn shelves at the back of the store, sniffing each other warily, like dogs recalling beatings. Whenever a pair connected and sidled out the door, they looked less excited than defeated.

Then one day a customer all but skipped up to the register. He was my age, with spiky hair and wittily highwater jeans, beaming an unapologetic grin. After he bought his books (*Giovanni's Room*, *The Thief's Journal*), he told me to meet him across the street, at the public library men's room (didn't ask me, *told* me—how did he know?). I begged my boss for a coffee break, bolted across Boylston, and made it back to work in twenty minutes. I had feared I'd find it gross or crumple up with guilt, but mostly what I felt was a dazzled sense of windfall. This stranger, like some passing sprite, had granted me a wish and flown away.

A month later, another guy. This one on the Esplanade. I'd been taking an after-work walk, a longcut home. (Had I heard talk about the Esplanade? I guess I must have. Active enough, but safer than the Fens—fewer muggings.) We caught each other's eyes, then ducked behind a bush, where I stood, moaning, while his blue-jeaned knees got soaked with mud.

Only a couple after that—both in the library bathroom—each so quick, I thought, it couldn't leave a mark.

Thomas had wondered what could be the point in pleasing strangers, but what I found was that I wasn't focused on the other men, whose names I rarely bothered to discover; the stranger I discovered was myself. A guy would bite my earlobes, or lick my underarms, and suddenly I was someone who ached for that. The mansion where my pleasures lived had so many more rooms than I'd imagined.

I told myself it was my own business. Nothing to do with Thomas. Certainly not with anything he lacked.

Told myself, too, that I was gathering material (and scribbled all the details in my journal). A writer had to brave the big, wide world.

Why, then, did I fail to tell Jim about my exploits? Jim, who shared these itches—for both sex and writing—and who, I knew, would have loved to sift through every hookup? *Because* he would; he'd want to make them evidence of something. I was unprepared to do that yet.

The day I got caught, Thomas was doing fieldwork at Plum Island, mapping phragmites stands in the Great Marsh. Said he wouldn't get back before seven. Plenty of time, I figured, to bring home the Belgian pilot who cruised me as I rang him up at Glad Day. Never before had I considered inviting someone home, but the pilot, in his smart Sabena cap and dark-blue blazer, glinting gold stripes on each cuff, looked so neat, so civilized, it wouldn't do to suck each other off in some foul stall.

When Thomas walked in, almost an hour early, we'd just showered; the pilot was wrapped in Thomas's terry robe. As soon as he had his pants on, I shoved the stranger out, then pelted Thomas with apologies, all of them clichés, even though, at the time, I believed them: "I don't even know his name. I'll never see him again. It meant nothing to me. Not a thing."

Thomas asked if I had ever done something like this before.

"No," I swore. "Of course not. I wouldn't." If "something like this" meant bringing a man home, I wasn't lying.

"Tell me at least you were safe, okay? Please? Were you safe?"

"Jesus, yes! You think I'm nuts? When I see what's happened to Jim?"

The specter of Jim, of his dying, made our fight seem smaller. Thomas stormed off and shut himself in the bedroom.

The next day, he rifled through my desk (how could I blame him?) and found my journal's chronicle of hookups. "Liar!" he said. "You lied. You promised me you never."

"But no," I said. "I thought you meant . . . I thought . . ." I couldn't go on. Thomas's face, his forthright face, had fallen in on itself. Here was this man I loved so much, this man I'd made my life with. Nothing but decent, handsome, and truehearted. What had I done? What had I done to him?

The shame of it stormed back through me now as I tore down the highway. Senselessly I stomped my foot. The Nova lurched ahead—just as a hulking Hood Milk truck changed lanes and cut me off.

I jammed the brakes, fishtailed to a stop along the shoulder, then sat clasping my chest, hardly breathing. Grateful to have dodged such a violent comeuppance (and only for a foolish, fleeting instant disappointed).

When I was finally calmed enough to get back on the road, I found I could barely shift the Nova into first. Second was worse—like tugging a pole through petrified molasses.

I thought about pulling off the road to find a phone, to call Dean and warn him I'd be late, but if I stopped, I worried, the car might never move again. I hugged the breakdown lane, hazards clacking.

The trip to Portland, normally less than two hours, took more than four.

By the time I walked through Jim's door, brimming with my trip's drama, it was nearly half past nine o'clock. "I'm *so* sorry. You wouldn't believe," I said. "My transmission—"

"Shh," said Jim. "You're wrecking it." His hospital bed was cranked way up. He looked as perky as I had seen in weeks.

Before him pranced Dean, in a T-shirt, tighty-whities, and leather chaps three inches too long for him. Stamping and twirling, he played at being a pouty supermodel, the chaps dragging the floor like a misguided mopping apparatus.

"Nice," Jim rasped, his voice hoarse with the aftermath of thrush.

The place was still polluted with its ghastly deathbed details: the mortar shell of an oxygen tank, the grease-scented suppositories (morphine made Jim harshly constipated), and Jim himself, skeletal, swallowed by the mattress, his scaly, fungal left foot protruding from the bedsheet as if impatient to wear a coroner's toe tag. And yet, here too was trampish Dean—a little leathered jester.

"What do you think, Ben?" said Jim. "I'm giving him my chaps."

I thought Dean looked dumb. Thought the chaps should go to *me*. Not that I would ever wear them—I wasn't into leather—but Dean and everyone else should know: I was the rightful heir.

"Least I can do," Jim added, "since he missed his big date."

"Sorry," I said again to Dean. "Maybe you could call the guy right now? Salvage something?"

Dean tossed me a haughty look and spun around again.

"Told him I'd be fine," said Jim. "Couple of hours alone? But no, he wouldn't dream of abandoning me, etcetera. Know what I think? I think he chickened out."

"Did *not*," said Dean, a little too fast and firm.

To me, he always looked even younger than eighteen. His flossy hair and fine-boned nose, even the fluffy way he walked—all of him seemed recently invented. He'd come to Jim's first as just the flower-delivery boy, twice a week bringing ostentatious sprays of roses, ordered by a mega-selling novelist pal of Jim's who felt bad for never visiting. Initially, Dean would stand in the hall and hand the flowers over, but on his third or fourth trip, Jim invited him in, and Dean stayed, chatting, for an hour. Soon he started making Jim's delivery his last of the day, so he could sit and talk through the evening. Jim would keep him rapt with epic tales of the good and bad old days—the Safeway in the Castro that sold Crisco by the gallon; the week in August '85 when four, count 'em, four, of his friends died—while Dean rubbed lotion into his feet.

"Isn't he just divoon?" said Jim after one visit. "If that's the future, I can croak in peace."

I tried not to snicker. Instead I asked, "The kid isn't exactly *sexy*, is he?" Dean's skin was spookily pale, akin to white asparagus; his storkish limbs were avant-garde sculptures. And yet there was something undeniably captivating in the way all his disparate parts converged—and, above all, in his newness. He brought to mind a pair of immaculate tennis shoes: you half wanted to keep him clean, half yearned to scuff and chafe and scar him.

"I don't know," Jim answered. "I find him compelling, for sure, but he's a skinny little creature, right? Almost looks like he has a touch of the AIDS."

I burped a single, skittish "Ha"; the joke had landed well wide of the mark.

Just how wide we'd learn as we got to know Dean better: he had come out at sixteen, in a fury of self-assurance (a one-man ACT UP branch at Biddeford High School), but he lived in such terror of contracting

HIV that he was still essentially a virgin. An occasional circle jerk with his teenage activist pals; a condomed blow job, once, from a flower-shop client; but Dean had never genuinely made love.

Which was why Jim pushed him hard to welcome every comer, even a mammoth-handed—and reportedly not too bright—lobster packer. "Educational," he'd told Dean. "Consider it gay college." (Dean was taking a gap year now, saving up to enroll at UMaine.)

But Dean seemed unready to fulfill Jim's ambitions for him—as unready as his legs were to fill out Jim's chaps.

"Shouldn't you have them hemmed?" I teased. "You can't meet your hunky lobster manhandler like *that*."

I thought I'd only meant to rib, but Dean must have detected my undertone of miffedness.

"Really?" he said. "Really? *You're* gonna give me dating advice? The guy who got so busted by his boyfriend?"

I was still rattled from my guilty thoughts of Thomas and also from the near miss with the milk truck. "You little twit," I said. "You don't know a fucking thing about it."

"Hey, hey—go easy," cautioned Jim.

Dean whined, "*He* started it. And he's the one who came two hours late."

"I tried to tell you, my car. My goddamn car broke down!"

"Boys," said Jim. "Please. My head is killing me. Please."

Immediately we both shushed. We scurried conscientiously. "What can I get you? Water?" I asked. Dean said, "Need some aspirin?"

"I need," said Jim, his voice abruptly despondent. "I need to rest."

~

The next day, as noon approached, Jim was still dozing. I had been waiting for him to get up, wanting to apologize, or thinking I should want to.

I'd slept ten full hours myself but woke up only all the more depleted. To make things worse (or maybe this was why I felt so tired), my sinuses were practically swollen shut. The culprit was an immense arrangement of calla lilies, which Dean had left in place of the usual roses. I tried not to think he'd known what they'd do to me.

Checking to see Jim's eyes were closed, I tiptoed to his desk and got some scissors. One by one, I snipped the lilies' pollen-swollen stamens and caught them in a plastic garbage bag.

Betty had come up early to do some cleaning, and now she watched me. Despite her bluish hair and its stuffy, upswept style (Jim had lately taken to calling her the Iron Lady), she could still come across as winningly pixieish. I shot her a look that begged for silence, and she pretended to twist a tiny key beside her mouth.

But then: *Clang! Clang!*

We turned to find Jim pounding against his bed rail. "What the fuck?" he yelled. "What do you think you're doing?"

"Sorry, I just," I started to say, but Betty stepped between us.

"James Baxter, you watch your mouth! And thank your stars for Ben. You know the grief he goes through just to come up here and help you?" (I'd told her about my near-death experience on the highway.)

"Yes, Ma, I know," said Jim. "But that's not his problem. He's mad at Dean, 'cause Dean got something he didn't."

"Am *not*," I said, sounding too much like Dean the night before. "I'm not mad at him. Mad at *you*." I hadn't quite let myself feel it until I said it.

"Ah," said Jim, "now we're getting somewhere."

"It's not fair," I said. "It's just not fair. Dean goes on and on about some stupid lobster packer, who's wrong for him in a dozen obvious ways, and all you do is grin and egg him on. But any time I mention Thomas—"

"Jesus, here we go," said Jim.

"Any time I mention him, you start taking potshots. Have you ever said anything encouraging?"

When Thomas had announced he was moving to California, I had finally confessed to Jim the whole unseemly story and shared my plan to get back in Thomas's good graces. Rather than consoling me, Jim had grown surly. He sniped at me erratically—sometimes about the way I was "groveling" to Thomas, other times about my supposedly clumsy nursing (I "stomped too loud" around his bed, except when I was "being so fucking creepy, just *standing* there"). I figured I deserved his abuse. That I had waited so long to confide must have hurt him. Also, I was sure, he was jealous. All along, I'd claimed I would sleep with only Thomas, but actually I had cheated—with random strangers, not Jim.

Jim asked me now to prop his neck with a fresh pillow. When he was settled, he said, "Okay, first off, about Dean? About Dean and this lunk he wants to fuck? The kid is just *eighteen*, Ben. The whole point of being eighteen is to fuck the wrong people."

"Jimmy! What did I say about your mouth?" Betty scolded, but both of us pointedly ignored her.

"And I'm twenty-three. So?" I said. "I'm already over the hill?"

"No," said Jim. "God, no—you're still so fucking young. You and Dean *both*—this is when you *need* to make mistakes. What's that saying? A hot-air balloon can only rise two ways: turn up the gas or toss away your ballast."

"Huh?" I said. "What does that even mean?"

Jim just closed his eyes, then let his head loll back, as if admiring his aphoristic wisdom.

Or no, maybe his pain had spiked. He suddenly looked shatterable.

"Tell me," he said tiredly. "Tell me about Thomas. What makes him so irreplaceable?"

It was a question I'd never really considered needing to answer. What makes *oxygen* irreplaceable?

Jim, despite his fondness for improbable romantic plots, had always doubted Thomas's and my future. How could a couple who'd gotten together as freshmen ever last? But wasn't that just bitterness on his part? When he had been an undergrad, all the queers were closeted; any chance for young love had been robbed.

"His loyalty?" I tried. I feared my answer sounded lame (how loyal was it of Thomas to have fled to San Francisco?), but I wasn't sure how else to explain it. "He's the one," I tried again, "who knows me now, who 'gets' all this"—I gestured to Jim's apartment, but what I meant was gayness, AIDS, grief, leather chaps—"but also knows exactly where I came from."

Jim, with considerable effort, propped himself on his elbows. He glared at me with priestly zeal, as if his bed were a pulpit. "Okay, fine.

Fine, then. Instead of constantly *moaning* about him, *go* to him. Go out there."

"What?" I said, so truly shocked I almost lost my balance. "Jim, you know I . . . obviously, I can't."

"I know no such thing. Why obviously?"

"For starters, you know I don't have that kind of money." I was barely surviving on the minimum wage at Glad Day, especially given all the shifts I'd skipped to tend to Jim, and I could ill afford to miss more. And now, too, the fucking Nova: How would I ever scrape together the funds to get it fixed? "Plus, I couldn't leave you," I said. "Not when you're, you know . . ."

"Course you could," he said. "You need a break."

"No," I said. "If someone deserves a long break, it's Betty."

"Me?" she said, arranging herself proudly in her armchair. "A day at the dog track's all I need. A cold beer and my betting sheet."

Jim smiled at his mother, then shot a tighter, taunting grin at me. "Maybe you're not so different from Dean. You *scared* to go? You chicken?"

"Bullshit," I said. "You don't know Thomas. He would never let me fly out there only just to dump me." Actually, what I did fear—what I thought I feared—was that I would ask Thomas if he wanted me to visit, and he would tell me no, please don't come.

Jim said, "Okay. Maybe you're scared he *will* take you back."

I couldn't even allow myself to digest what he'd said, let alone manage a response.

"Go," he said. "It's the only way: go out and see him. Book the trip on Delta. Use my miles."

"Whoa," I said. "Seriously?" A punchy laugh spilled out of me. "Sure this isn't just the morphine talking?"

"I mean it," he said. "More than enough for a first-class flight. They're yours."

His shift had happened so fast, I could barely follow it, or figure out how to feel about it. Guardedly, I edged myself onto Jim's bed, giving the mattress only half my weight. "I don't get it," I said. "Suddenly you've stopped hating him?"

"Ben, I've never hated him. I've never even met him." He seemed about to say something more but had to pause to cough; he hacked up a glob of grayish phlegm. Wincing, he said, "Sorry . . . but speaking of the morphine. Could we maybe, please? Is it time?"

We weren't supposed to give him his new patch until that evening. I looked to Betty, who shrugged and said, "What, he'll get addicted?" Then she clapped her hands twice. "And I can change *mine*, too!" Her patch was NicoDerm. In solidarity with Jim, and in deference to his oxygen tanks, she was trying to kick her two-packs-a-day habit.

"Fine," I said, pulling out Jim's morphine from its wrapper. "Just be careful you don't mix up the patches."

"You *bet* I'd quit smoking, if I got *his* patch," said Betty. "Who needs cigs if you're high as a hundred kites?"

"Ha," I said. "Jim would get the raw deal if you switched. But maybe—"

"Shit," said Jim. He glared at his lap. "I've got to go. I'm going."

"Want the urinal?"

"Fuck's sake, yes. Quick!"

He managed to aim most of his piss into the plastic jug, but still, a stain bloomed onto the sheets.

"Want me to change them?" I asked.

"Nah," he said. "Don't bother." He didn't sound embarrassed, just disheartened.

"Swear to God," said Betty, "if I have to do more laundry . . . Know what? I'm going to toss those sheets and buy more. Going to K-Mart."

"Our thrifty Yankee forebears are spinning in their graves," said Jim.

"Yuh," she said, "they never dealt with AIDS. Let 'em spin." Hefting her big brown pocketbook—less a purse than a toolbox—she bolted up, as if her dose of nicotine were rocket fuel.

It was not uncommon for her to dash away like this. I was never sure if she was simply being no-nonsense, getting her errands finished while she could, or if she vanished to hide her grief from Jim. This time, as she walked to the door, she sent me a private look, and I understood she wanted to give me time alone with him.

"Know what I think? I don't think he hates Thomas," she said. She'd stopped at the threshold and turned to me, but her voice was aimed at Jim. "Don't you think he hates that he's not Thomas?"

Out she went, with a brisk, sturdy tug of the door behind her, the prudent clomp of her pumps down the stairs.

I had been so flustered by Jim's gift of the Delta miles that I had missed its obvious implications. He was finally letting go of his pipe dreams for good. Letting go even of the pretense.

I smoothed his shoulder's flaccid skin, trying to get the morphine patch to stick. "You're giving up? Really?" I said.

"It's not me. It's my body."

"But no, what Betty was saying. You hoped to take me from Thomas, but the fight's done—he wins, he can have me?"

Traffic on the street below, the glum chuckle of rubber tires on cobbles. Here, inside: the anemic air; Jim's halting breaths; all the sharp and creamy smells of sickness.

"Ben," said Jim, "I'm not sure you really understand." His eyes were dark, at once hard and yielding. "Know why people liked my books," he said, "and bought so many?" He drew a shredded breath, then fell into a coughing fit. Coughed so hard that tears came to his eyes.

I turned on his oxygen and pressed the mask to his face. Finally his breathing calmed and he pushed the mask away. Urgently I thumbed drops of sweat off his temple, as if I could stem a larger flood.

"Wasn't the smutty parts," he said. "What they liked was my heroes. I made them flawed, and pushed them hard, way past where they ever dreamed of going. But always—*always*—I gave the hero a happy ending. Trust me, okay? And trust yourself. You're going to go so far."

I'd never cried. Not here, anyway. Not in front of Jim. Not even when I'd asked him, the visit before last—a day he seemed to billow with a warm, frisky wind—if he might want a notebook and a pen, to jot his thoughts, and he'd said, "Oh, God, no. I'm done with words."

But this. The term *hero*, with its bold, ambitious ring. That Jim had seemed to bestow it now on me.

Not wanting him to see my tears, I climbed into bed beside him, buried my face against his bony shoulder. At first he cringed—almost any touch, these days, caused pain—but soon he relaxed and reached across and softly stroked my head. His fingers traced my ear's curve, a whisper of a touch. Again and again, every time softer.

His chest's cycle of rise and fall slowed to almost nothing. His hand went limp, then twitched alert, then traced my ear again.

I pressed harder against him, lips to dry skin. His body was so suddenly old. So old and small—*diminished*. But it was beautiful, too, maybe more than ever, its tough and fragile systems pulsing nearer to the surface. The closer his death, the more aware I was of his still-aliveness. To touch him—even now, atop his sweaty sickbed—felt like tapping into something endless.

"Jim . . . ," I said. I wanted to tell him how much I would miss him. My throat tightened; nothing would come out. And then I . . . did I really?

I got a hard-on.

If I could, I'd beam myself back onto that bed. I'd take Jim's diminished hand and wrap it around my cock. *See?* I'd say. *For you! That's how much I feel.*

I was confused. I knew no category for our bond. It wasn't like with Thomas, who made me earn his love, who might revoke it, depending on how nobly I behaved. Jim loved me for who I was, it seemed, not what I did. For no reason other than that he loved me.

I rolled away, embarrassed, hoping he'd felt no change. "Jim?" I said.

It didn't matter. He was gently snoring.

~

Because my Nova was done for, Jim lent me his Chrysler, a big, black, barge-like New Yorker. Its gimmick was a naggy digital voice ("Please fasten your seatbelt!"), and Jim had come to fear the day, or so he'd often joked, when he would turn the key and hear "Don't get your AIDS all over my steering wheel."

I rushed home to Boston, eager to call Thomas—who, when I explained Jim's gift ("Ninety-seven thousand miles"), said, "Wow, that's generous. Where do you think you'll go?"

"Oh, come on, Thomas," I said.

"What? You could go anywhere."

"The only place I want to go," I said, "is where you are."

He let a long silence pass. At last he said, "And what does Jim expect to get from you?"

As stung as Thomas was by my infidelities, I don't think he worried I'd sleep with Jim. He knew my tastes ran to younger, brawny guys, and plus, now, he knew how sick Jim was. But maybe the lack of a sexual explanation for my love of Jim threatened Thomas all the more acutely. Hard enough to forgive me for the strangers, the "nothing" sex. But Jim, he knew, kept me on the hook with something else—something he must have sensed he couldn't give me.

"Jim expects me to do what makes me happy," I said. "That's all."

Another long silence.

Through my thin bedroom wall, I listened to my housemates—all five of them—in the kitchen, playing poker. When Thomas had left, I'd moved into a tenement of strangers.

Thomas started chatting about the beauty of Lagunitas Creek, where, just today, he'd seen otters, widgeons, teals. Then he segued, oddly, to a riff about the foods in San Francisco that he'd never known in Boston ("Thousand-year-old eggs! Beef-tongue tacos!").

I'd always loved the way he ate—so ravenous, so boyish—and as he talked, I could picture the muscles of his jaw, the macho nodes that bulged out when he chewed. Could I recall any of my hookups a *tenth* so clearly? Why would I have risked for them all I had with Thomas?

". . . and also," he was saying, "there's the 'wave organ,' okay? Down at the Marina, made of PVC pipes. The tide comes in, and it sounds like . . . well, I guess you'll see."

"Wait," I said. "Slow down a sec. Slow down. Is that a yes?"

"Yes," he said, laughing, "that's a yes."

"Oh!" I said. "Oh, Thomas. I'll try not to disappoint you." I kissed the phone receiver and said, "I love you."

"Love you, too," he said—the first time in weeks he'd used the word. "And hey, when you see him, tell Jim thanks."

~

I never had the chance to tell Jim that or anything else.

The next three days, every time I called, he was sleeping. (I had to stay in Boston; my boss would can me if I didn't take some shifts.) Then, the fourth morning, at eight o'clock, the phone rang. "It's over," said Dean. "Sorry, Ben. He's gone."

My horrid, childish, unspeakable thought: Why does *Dean* get to be there?

I asked if Betty was with him.

"She is. She's with his body."

Better, I thought. But still. "Wait," I said. "I'll come right up. I'm coming." I got dressed and ran out to the car.

I turned the key ("Please fasten your seatbelt!") and took hold of the wheel, my head filling with Jim's jokey voice: "Don't get your AIDS all over my steering wheel." A single, stony fist of laughter punched up through my throat. Then came rage, and loneliness, and I was shouting: "Fuck! Fuck! Fuck!"

I barreled north at ninety, loathing the drivers who blocked my way. *Jim is dead, Jim is dead*, my mind's siren blared. The deluge of adrenaline was sick-making but satisfying, like booze chugged to numb a broken bone.

I'd never seen a dead body—not one that hadn't yet been fixed up for a wake. I wanted to see Jim's eyes again, his pebbly, probing eyes, but also couldn't help but hope I would find them closed. What should I do? Hold his bloodless hand? Kiss his fingers?

Jim had told me once about the day Kurt had died. Kurt had been his one great love; they'd lived together, for four years, when Jim was in his thirties, in New York. When Jim came home one afternoon from a book signing in Brooklyn, Kurt had taped a note at eye level on their door: "Jim—don't light any cigarettes."

"Knew right away, of course," Jim said. "I knew."

They'd both tested positive for HIV a year before, getting their results the same day, but recently Kurt had convinced himself—why, Jim wasn't sure—that *he* was to blame, that he had infected Jim.

He found Kurt in the kitchen, his head on the open oven door. "Looked like he was laughing," said Jim. "His mouth all stiff and wide. 'Close it,' I wanted to yell at him. 'Close your mouth. Shut the fuck up!'"

I was still slamming past the cars on I-95. Just as I crossed the New Hampshire line, I glimpsed, along the highway's side, a stiffened squirrel, muddy with its own blood. It skittered in a semi's wake, as negligible as trash. Dead, I thought; Jim is dead. What was I speeding for?

I drove the rest of the way at sixty-five.

~

I found Betty positioned, as usual, in the armchair, her lap filled with photographs of Jim. Her right hand fiddled with a button on Jim's mattress (the underpad and bedding had been stripped), and her left held a lit cigarette. "The mortuary men," she said, "were nice. Took him away." She drew a long, wheezing drag of smoke. "But it was all so fast. So fast." She meant the men, the speed with which they carried off Jim's corpse, but just as well could have meant the life shown in the photos: toddler in a cowboy hat, swaggering high school grad, AIDS activist bellowing through a bullhorn.

I couldn't talk, all choked up with letdown and relief at the fact that his body had been taken. The air was sickly sweet with a fetid, fecal smell, but still, that scent was Jim's—his body had produced it—and so I wanted to breathe it all in.

Dean came in from the kitchen with a mighty floral arrangement: white roses and asters, eucalyptus. He set the vase on the nightstand, beside ten sets of sheets—the whole stack still factory-sealed in plastic—and greeted me with a sharp, ribby hug.

"I should've been here," I said.

"Wish you were," said Dean. He seemed both more needy and more knowing than before. His ghostly skin looked fitting for the occasion. He readjusted an aster, then undid what he'd changed. "So," he said, "what do we do now?"

Jim had drawn up such precise instructions for his funeral—the Frank O'Hara poem to read, the finger food to serve—that there was little work left for us. Betty had called Jim's siblings and the local *Times* stringer (a friend of Jim's who'd promised he would lobby for an obit). His rooms would need a good scrubbing, but not yet. Not yet.

"Why don't you just rest," I said. "Both of you. You need it. I'm going to try and tidy up Jim's desk." There was nothing to tidy, of course; he hadn't worked in months. But maybe if I lingered in his chair, I'd still feel him.

As I approached the desk, Betty called from behind me, "Oh, that's right. Meant to tell you, Ben, a package came—"

But I had already found it, ripped it open.

Dear Mr. Baxter:

We're happy to help you give the gift of travel!

> To complete the mileage transfer to your designated recipient, bring the enclosed Transfer Certificate to any Delta counter. An authorized representative will witness your signature . . .

I read the rest through fogging eyes. Jim had given me so much—not least, my start in writing—but now he'd never give me these miles or any other thing.

My thoughts ashamed me; I should mourn Jim, not my own lost prospects. (It took me years to understand that that's what mourning is: the pain not only of missing someone else's lost potential but of losing what he could have been, and could have done, for *you*.)

The page was shaking. Someone's hands were shaking it. My hands.

I must have made a sound; Dean rushed over and put his weedy arm around my shoulders. "Jim was so excited," he said, "to give you all these miles. He made me call Delta the other day, to make it happen."

"Oh, well," I said. My voice was thin. "Easy come, easy go."

"Wait—why do you say that?"

"He has to sign it. In person." I summarized the letter's strict instructions.

"No, come on. They'll understand." He took the form and scrutinized it, as though his young, entitled gaze could change its legalese. "Let's go down to the airport," he said.

"Now?" I said. "We can't."

"What's there to do here, except just being sad?"

Maybe that was all we were supposed to do, I thought. "But Betty," I said.

"She won't mind. Or she can come along."

Before I could urge him not to, he asked her what she wanted.

"Go," she said. "Go on."

"You sure you'll be okay?" I said.

"Yuh. Actually, I think I'd like to be alone for a bit."

I scanned the dim apartment, a study in futility. The pristine, folded sheets; the empty plastic urinals; on a shelf, unopened, a box of morphine patches: comfort for pain Jim was now beyond.

Dean placed the Delta letter back into my hands. "Come on, it'll be like one of Jim's god-awful jokes: 'My Best Friend Went to Heaven, and All I Got Were His Lousy Airline Miles.'"

"You can't be serious," I said. "You think he went to *heaven*?"

"Touché," said Dean. "I didn't mean to doubt him."

~

We drove Jim's New Yorker to the airport. Liberated from the morbid apartment, Dean grew quickly hyper, buzzing with plans for how to win the miles. "Want me to cry? I'm killer at crying on cue," he said. "I am! Last week a statie pulled me over doing seventy-nine. I bawled so hard, he gave me just a warning."

"No," I said. "Be normal, all right? I don't want a scene."

"Oh, now, Ben," he said with forbearing condescension—a tone, I thought, inherited from Jim. "Okay, fine. How about we say Jim's still alive but just too sick to come down in person?"

"Please . . . please, don't" was all I managed. A fragile feeling muzzled me, my mouth chalky with one crumbled sentence after another.

"You're just asking for what he tried to give you," Dean insisted. "If you were his *wife*, would there be any question?"

"I wasn't even his boyfriend," I said, and grief pinched again: not because I had never been Jim's beloved but because *he* had ended up alone. Or maybe what I felt was fear, the fear that made me so focused on flying out to Thomas: How would I feel if I were no one's lover?

We crossed the Fore River and approached the Portland Jetport, a throwback of an airport, no bigger than most elementary schools. We parked in the windswept, nearly vacant lot.

"What do you think it was like for Jim?" I asked. "Dying alone?"

"What do you mean? He had Betty. He had us."

"But after Kurt," I said as we walked toward the terminal. "*Alone* alone. You think he wanted a boyfriend?"

Dean pondered this. "Maybe, but he didn't believe in boyfriends for their own sake—not, you know, as a shortcut to being happy. He would say that you have to be happy first, by yourself."

"But all these years in Portland," I said, "he hardly even dated, despite being 'the famous erotic writer.' Don't you think he must've felt . . . I don't know, like a vegetarian writing bacon cookbooks?"

A kind of emotional weather seemed to pass across Dean's eyes: a tumble of clouds, then, all of a sudden, sun. "No," he said. "It wasn't like that. You know what it was like? Like Beethoven! Writing symphonies after he went deaf." The terminal door slid open, and he went marching through.

Who was this Dean, so suddenly wise and soulfully self-assured? Now I saw in him what Jim must have seen. I hustled after him, fortified with something that felt like faith.

My hopes continued rising as we neared the Delta counter and I caught sight of the staffer on duty: a high-hipped man of a certain age, his every feature a tick too self-conscious. Mustache clipped like topiary, orchidesque pocket square in perfect starchy bloom. "Think we're in luck," I whispered to Dean.

"Oh, for sure, she's *family*."

The man looked up, his mouth pulled tight. He couldn't have heard us, could he?

Flashing a smile of fellowship, I swished forth, apology in my eyes. "Sorry to bother," I said, and pulled out the certificate. "My friend Jim, he got this, so I could have his miles, and—"

"Sorry, I'll stop you there." His frown was mild, professional. "The miles holder has to sign in person."

"Yeah, I know," I said. "I know that's what the rules say, but . . ." Now was when I'd have to utter *Jim* and *dead* together. I couldn't. My throat was made of tar.

"If Mr."—he tilted his head, in order to read the form—"if Mr. Baxter desires to gift the miles, it's quite simple. He—"

"Look," said Dean. "Obviously, Jim was planning to give him the miles."

"Wait," said the man suspiciously (had he noted Dean's past-tense verb?). "If the miles holder's *deceased*, the certificate is invalid. And then there's nothing—"

"What?" I said. "How *dare* you?" Jim was gone, yes, but for this officious stranger to guess that fact so brusquely, to render Jim so breezily extinct? "Who said Jim was dead?" I said. "How could you even think that?" I looked to Dean, who got my message: *Okay, fine, let's fib.*

"You really think we'd come here, if our friend was dead, and *lie*?" said Dean.

The staffer raised his chin as if to a far-off fanfare. "Fraud is something *you* may not have to think about, but *we* do."

Tuttle (so said his name tag) offered to phone Jim, but I said no, he couldn't, Jim was too ill to talk—inflecting *ill*, I hoped, with an intimation of AIDS.

"But Betty," I said. "Jim's mother. She knows the miles are mine."

Dean interrupted. "Sorry—is there a bathroom?"

I glared at him. How could he abandon me right now?

"There," said Tuttle, pointing. "Just beyond the gift shop."

"Thanks," said Dean, and caught my eye. Something in his widened gaze said *Stall for a minute. Trust me.*

Of course. He would try to get to Betty.

Tuttle wondered aloud why he should bother to call "the mother"—how could he even know that's who she was—but seemed to have lost his zeal for rigid rule-enforcing.

I stalled as long as I could, making a show of fishing for Jim's number in my wallet, even though, of course, I knew it by heart. Finally, I read it out to Tuttle, then waited while he dialed, nervousness like static in my ears.

"Busy," he said, and hung up. I thought he sounded relieved. "Tell her to call corporate, okay? Maybe they'll make an exception."

"Just wait," I said. "Can't you please just wait and try again?"

Tuttle shrugged unreadably; he wouldn't meet my eyes.

His blankness tipped me over the edge again. "Haven't you ever dealt with someone sick before?" I said. "Someone too sick to handle all this shit?"

Tuttle recoiled. He touched his mustache corners with his thumbs, as if measuring the width of his whole world, and when he finally looked at me—such sadness in his stringent eyes—I was forced to see what I had missed. A queen like him, I realized, a man of Tuttle's age? Probably he had lost a dozen friends, perhaps a lover. And here I'd made a mockery of Jim's death (was that what Tuttle thought?), fighting for miles instead of properly mourning. Or maybe he was infected and imagining his own death. Maybe he knew that no one—no lover, or friend like me—would fight to claim the legacy he would leave.

"Sorry," I said. "So sorry. That was out of line." I longed to reach across to him, to stroke his dainty jaw.

Tuttle dialed again. Something had been wrung out of him, it seemed. "Mrs. Baxter?" I heard him say. "Forgive me for intruding . . ."

Would Betty make the distinction, as Jim had always done, between a story's facts and its truth? The truth in the lie we asked of her: Jim did want to give me his miles, in order to push me toward my happy ending. (I pictured me and Thomas, standing at the Pacific, salted wind sluicing through our hair.)

"Well," said Tuttle, hanging up, his eyes a little soggy, "the situation is highly unconventional. Against my better judgment, I'll say yes."

"Oh!" I said. "Thank you. I can't thank you enough."

Just then Dean loped back, floaty on his toes. "Everything good?" he asked.

I just smiled.

Tuttle said he'd send a special note up to corporate; we should get confirmation next week. "Best of luck," he said, "with your friend's illness." He bent his head and started clacking away at the computer.

Dean and I darted through the terminal, saying nothing, as if a single syllable might pierce the moment's membrane and everything would suddenly deflate. Out we dashed, across the parking lot to Jim's New Yorker, slammed the doors, and then, in the car's sanctuary, squealed and shrieked and fell against each other.

"Jesus, that was close!" I said.

"We should scram," said Dean, "before he changes his mind."

But when I tried to start the car, the engine only whined.

"Shit," I said, and tried again: another feeble sound.

"Your battery is low," bossed the car's robotic voice. "Prompt service is required."

"What the fuck?" I said. "Could I have left the lights on?"

I don't think Dean heard me; he had collapsed in laughter. "Service me," he barked in a stiff but sultry voice, like some kind of automated porn star. "Prompt service! I need to be serviced now!"

It wasn't really funny, but I was laughing, too. I bent down and pantomimed giving Dean a blow job.

"Know who gives good service?" he said. "Tuttle. What a whore!"

The thought of Tuttle slutting around made us both laugh harder. I felt my eyes fattening with tears. "Oh, it's so fucked-up," I said. "What a fucked-up day."

"Imagine, though," said Dean, "how Jim would've *loved* this."

"You're right," I said.

He lifted an imaginary glass. "To Jim!"

"To Jim," I said.

We made our knuckles clink.

~

On the phone that night, I said the same to Thomas: how cheered Jim would've been, if only he could've seen us; how his spirit had seemed to hover above the whole caper. I'd given Thomas the play-by-play—the struggle with Tuttle; Dean's Hail Mary sprint to find a pay phone; Betty's magnanimous response ("Actually, she seemed to get a chuckle out of it all. Like something out of her spy novels, she said")—and I could sense Thomas's astonishment through the phone. The lengths I'd gone to get the miles to bring us back together!

"Almost like Jim planned it from beyond the grave," I said. "That would be just like him, wouldn't it?"

"Ben," said Thomas, "how *could* you?"

The blade of his voice. I bled before I knew it.

"What do you mean?" I managed to say. "You feel bad for Delta? Trust me, I think they'll be just fine."

"I don't give a damn about Delta," Thomas scoffed. "But Betty—her son's just died, her son's at the crematorium, and you make her pretend he's alive?"

Dense, dismal silence on the line.

Meekly, I muttered, "This was what Jim wanted."

"Really? To make his mother lie? And you—for *you* to lie?"

"Oh, come on. It wasn't really—"

"It *is*, Ben. It's lying. That's all you seem good at anymore."

I was sitting at Jim's desk, above which, on two packed shelves, sat copies of all his books: *The Married Man. Flesh of My Flesh. For the Lust of Pete: A Romance.* I swiveled in his chair, the chair in which he'd dreamed up all those filthy, funny tales—stories where the leading man hurdled every bar to find his bliss.

The chair squeaked. A similar noise came scritching through the phone. On what sort of chair did Thomas sit in San Francisco? What was his view: A sparkling sky? An airshaft's bleak brick wall? For five years, we had seen and done everything together. I knew all his private sounds—asleep, on the john, fucking—and he knew all the same about me. But now, these past six months, we'd fashioned separate selves. What did we still know about each other?

"I did it for you," I said. "For *us*. Don't you see?"

Thomas's steady, steely breaths gave way to a quiet snort. "I never asked you to lie for me. I never would," he said. "All I've asked was for you to tell the truth."

My instinct was to apologize—I'd grown so used to telling Thomas sorry—but had I done anything all that wrong? A hard, upending thought occurred: Maybe I'd done the right thing but for the wrong person.

"It's late," I finally said. "I'll call you when the miles go through, all right?"

"All right," he said.

~

The funeral would be taking place in five days, a Tuesday: service at First Parish, reception at Jim's apartment (deviled eggs and extra-dirty Martinis, his favorites). Monday, as we tidied up the apartment, the phone rang.

"This is Mrs. Baxter," said Betty. "Who? Aha! Delta. I had such a lovely chat last week with one of your colleagues." She winked at me, and from her wrinkled eighty-something face beamed a buoyancy I recognized as Jim's. The source of Jim's.

Then "Oh," she said. "Oh, my. You saw it?" With what I read as panic, she pointed to the nightstand, on which, beneath Jim's photo, she'd placed his *Times* obit.

Fuck. So much for our fiction of keeping him alive.

Betty tried politeness, insisting we had not meant to dupe, but the conversation quickly turned contentious ("A *scam*? These were my *son's* miles—he *earned* them!"). She slammed down the phone.

I had gotten the gist, of course, but Betty told the rest: because our "fraudulent claim" had breached their "terms and conditions," Delta was going to nullify Jim's miles.

Now I wouldn't get them. No one would.

"Ridiculous, all this fuss," she said, "for something that isn't even real. *Hypothetical* miles."

It had been awful hearing her fight, hearing her be demeaned on my behalf. Maybe Thomas was right. Maybe this whole business was abasing.

I took her by both elbows and brought my face near hers. I said, "It *is* ridiculous. I'm sorry. Please, let's drop it. Please, can we—"

She raised her palm to shush me. "Jim left you those miles," she said, "but what did he leave me? *You*. Your friendship." She poked a stiff finger at my heart. "Now it's my job to fight for you. I'll get those GD miles."

~

Later, after Betty left (she wanted to sleep at home), I gathered all my strength and called Thomas. We hadn't spoken since our fight. I wondered if he felt as rotten as I did.

Maybe if I reported how Betty was going to bat for us, it would ease his mind about our scheme. Or maybe he'd be pleased to hear that we might lose the miles. Would that satisfy his sense of justice?

No answer.

At this hour, he might still be working at Point Reyes, pulling invasive pepperweed from the marsh.

I left a message: "Update on the miles. I'm at Jim's. Call me."

~

Dean stopped by after dinner, offering help for tomorrow. The place was already spick-and-span, the eggs had all been deviled—there was nothing much left to do—but I disliked the thought of being alone. I told him, "Stay."

I proposed we try out the gin I'd bought for the reception.

Dean said, "Tough job, but someone's got to do it."

Thinking we shouldn't make a mess of the newly gleaming kitchen, I poured us shots, doubles, in a couple of Dixie cups. We sat on the floor of Jim's office, sipping.

I told Dean of Betty's plan to deal with Delta's bullshit. As Jim's next of kin, she would inherit all he left—including, she would argue, his miles. Which, once she got them, she'd hand right off to me. ("Bet they'll cave when my lawyer calls," she'd said.)

"Think it'll work?" asked Dean.

"Don't know. Guess it could." I gulped some gin: a flash behind my eyes. "Part of me thinks we should just forget it."

"Maybe you could ask Betty for Jim's car," he said. "Road trip all the way to California?"

"Maybe," I said. But why did I sense that that might miss the point? Why did I so badly want the *miles*? "Thomas and I are fighting again, but Jim would still say go, right? Fly out there and patch things up in person?"

Dean looked into my eyes. "You think *that's* what he wanted?"

"He practically ordered me to go to San Francisco!"

"Right," said Dean, "but that doesn't mean . . ." We were sitting cross-legged, facing each other, close. He looked down, then back into my eyes. "I wasn't supposed to say this, but . . . he hoped if you went to San Fran, you'd finally get it—get Thomas—out of your system."

"But no," I said, "Jim said to me . . ." What had he actually said? That I should go to Thomas, not why. "Wow," I said, "he really told you that?"

Dean scooched even closer, put a hand on my knee. "He said he'd never tell you directly, that you would have to figure it out yourself. He also loved goading you, though"—Dean was smiling now—"letting you think that he was just so crazy-jealous of Thomas. Said he knew you'd never give in but you'd feel crummy not to, and that was when you'd give him the most affection."

It was hard to absorb this new view of Jim and me. He had fooled me—or actually, he'd let me fool myself—but all by way of bringing us even closer.

"Did you ever?" I said.

"What?"

"Sleep with Jim?"

"No," he said, "but honestly? Now, I wish I had."

"Me, too, sort of," I said. "Jim was . . . he was really something, wasn't he?"

"Yeah," said Dean, "but that's not even really what I meant. I wish I'd said yes, 'cause I should say yes to everything. That was what he tried to make us see, don't you think? Never to shut out any chances?"

His voice induced a strange kind of lightness deep inside me. My bones felt feathery. I guessed the gin was working.

"Practically the last thing he said to me," said Dean, "was 'You'll be sorry you never let me fuck you.'"

"Wait," I said. "He used that line on *me*. The dirty dog!"

"Oh my God, too funny," said Dean. "Dirty, dirty dog."

"Lovable, though."

"Yeah," said Dean. "Nothing if not lovable."

I poured more gin, and we reprised the toast we'd made the other day, but now with actual cups, actual booze. "To Jim," we said, and tossed the doubles down.

The gin had full hold of me now, but I was far from fuzzy. Just the opposite: my thoughts were all rinsed clear. It felt like Jim had put me—put us—here.

Our kissing seemed inevitable, out of our control. Dean tasted cleanly of gin: piney, vivifying. He sucked my tongue in pulses, as if it were his thumb. His hair had a stale, homey smell.

As if by prearrangement, we stopped at the same instant, pulled apart and started sweetly laughing. I felt nothing close to my usual sexual hunger, just an easy, pleasant satisfaction. I'd liked the kiss but couldn't imagine wanting to kiss him more.

He smiled at me wholeheartedly. "Better just as brothers?"

"Yeah," I said. "Brothers. Absolutely."

We hugged hard, our foreheads pressed together.

The phone rang.

Since Dean was closer to Jim's desk, he got it. "Hey!" he said. "I've heard so much about you. He's right here."

I took the phone.

"It's late," said Thomas. "What's he doing there?"

I motioned to Dean for privacy, and he went off to the bedroom. "Oh, just our own little private wake," I said. "We're just mostly hanging out, I guess."

"'*Mostly* hanging out'?" he said. "You '*guess*'?"

"Well, and doing shots," I said. "Drinking toasts to Jim." It would've been the easiest thing to tell him nothing more. Leave it at that, and he'd never be the wiser. But Thomas wanted the truth, and now I wanted it, too. Needed it, despite what it would cost us, or because of that.

"Also, we were making out," I told him. "Me and Dean." I didn't claim that it had meant nothing.

Thomas didn't respond. I wondered if he'd hung up. But then I heard a muffled sniffle. "Ben?" he said.

"Yeah."

"Ben, why would you, when we were finally almost . . . why'd you do that?"

I didn't know, exactly, but not knowing felt okay. I needed the leeway to do the wrong things, maybe.

"What happened?" he said. "What happened to the Ben you used to be?" He cried this out, as though becoming someone new was bad.

Sometimes, in the coming months—as lonely as I had ever been—I would wonder if maybe he was right. Where was the happy ending Jim had crafted? But Jim's writing was shrewder than I gave him credit for. Reading his stories again now, I see his artful tricks, the ways he pushed against his genre's limits. Happy endings, yes, but different from what you'd guess. Satisfying, but not untinged by pain.

"Thomas," I said, "I'm sorry. I don't know what to tell you."

The phone line hummed like highway noise, the sound of the span between us.

Finally he said, "And what about the miles? What's the update?"

I told him of the Delta agent's threat, and Betty's plan.

"Oh," he said. "So you're not sure you'll get them after all?"

"No," I said. "I trust Betty. I know she's going to get them." As soon as the words came out, I was certain.

Through the phone: his breathing, that old, consoling sound. How would I say I probably wouldn't come to California? Maybe, for now, I wouldn't even cash in the miles, I thought. I would bank them, and rack up more, until I was ready to pick my route. There were so many places I could fly.

Acknowledgments

Some of the stories in this book first appeared, in earlier versions, in the following publications:

"Over Boy" in *Tin House* and *Bestial Noise: The Tin House Fiction Reader*
"You Are Here" in the *Southern Review* and *Best New American Voices 2005*
"Uncle Kent" in the *Louisville Review*
"Thieves" in *Guernica*
"Stud" in *Nerve* and *Smut: Volume 1*
"Do Us Part" in the *Kenyon Review*
"Marge" in *Post Road* and *Between Men: Best New Gay Fiction*

Heartfelt thanks to the editors of these publications, as well as to the scores of friends and colleagues who, in reading many drafts, over the course of many years, helped me improve these stories.

MICHAEL LOWENTHAL is the author of four novels: *The Same Embrace*, *Avoidance*, *Charity Girl*, and *The Paternity Test*. His short stories and essays have appeared in *Tin House*, *Ploughshares*, the *Southern Review*, the *Kenyon Review*, the *New York Times Magazine*, *True Story*, *Guernica*, and *The Rumpus*, and have been widely anthologized.

The recipient of fellowships from the Bread Loaf and Wesleyan writers' conferences, the MacDowell Colony, and the Mass Cultural Council, Lowenthal has taught creative writing at Boston College and Hampshire College, and as the Picador Guest Professor for Literature at Leipzig University. Since 2003, he has been a faculty member in the low-residency MFA in Creative Writing program at Lesley University.

Lowenthal lives in Boston and can be reached at www.MichaelLowenthal.com.